NEIL VICKERS

TRUE LOVE

UNLIMITED

First paperback edition

Ethan Fosse Publications
Ethan.fosse10@gmail.com

978-1-80227-426-4 (paperback)
978-1-80227-427-1 (ebook)

Preface

This romance thriller is about a man who boards the Eurostar train from St Pancras, London to Paris and a woman he meets who boards the same train at Calais, France. They exchange stories and passions throughout their time together that will end up in an epic journey full of action and mystery. A true love story but they are both running away from broken relationships or so it seems. Ending off in a dangerous twist of fate.

This book is dedicated to my sister, Susan Vickers 1953–1967

Contents

Chapter 1..9

Chapter 2...17

Chapter 3...21

Chapter 4...27

Chapter 5...31

Chapter 6...35

Chapter 7...39

Chapter 8...47

Chapter 9...53

Chapter 10...61

Chapter 11...69

Chapter 12...79

Chapter 13...87

Chapter 14...97

Chapter 15...105

Chapter 16...113

Chapter 17...121

Chapter 18...127

Chapter 19 135

Chapter 20 141

Chapter 21 145

Chapter 22 151

Chapter 23 155

Chapter 24 157

Chapter 25 163

Chapter 26 167

Chapter 27 175

Chapter 28 179

Chapter 29 185

Chapter 30 193

Chapter 31 199

Chapter 32 209

Chapter 33 215

Chapter 34 221

Chapter 35 225

Chapter 36 229

Chapter 37 235

Chapter 38 241

Chapter 39 245

Chapter 40 251

Chapter 41..257

Chapter 42..269

Chapter 43..277

Chapter 44..281

Chapter 45..285

Chapter 46..287

Chapter 47..293

Chapter 48..299

Chapter 49..303

Chapter 1

Mateo

As the sunlight came through the window, it made her long straight hair look like silk. Her hair was a deep black like the abyss in the ocean that sees no light. The carriage window was open slightly; her hair gently blowing and shimmering like the wing feather of a raven in flight. Her skin was a shade of olive. The sunlight through the window made her skin glimmer.

She was wearing a white blouse; it was so hot in the carriage she had loosened the top buttons to capture what coolness was left in the air. I could not stop looking as she fidgeted around to find a comfortable position. I needed to look away before I made her feel uncomfortable, but I was captivated by her beauty. I tried to keep looking at the fields as the train sped by, but my eyes were filled with the desire to see more. Looking over to see her thin red knee-length pencil skirt slightly open exposing her bare legs, soft and smooth like velvet, crossing them to change position. As she moved, she leant over and smiled.

She asked me, "How long is it to Paris?"

I replied, "Around three hours."

She smiled again and said, "Thank you."

My thoughts were running wild. Was that an introduction?

I smiled back and replied, "You're welcome."

I could feel the blood in my body pumping fast as a sweat bead formed above my forehead. I was excited but scared at the same time. I hoped the journey would go on forever so I could get to know her better.

Just then, the refreshment trolley arrived in the carriage and spoilt any chance of more conversation as she was looking in her bag for change. I looked away; my eyes were in love, I heard her order an expresso and a bottle of water. I wanted to pay for her drinks, but I stopped myself from asking as I did not even know her name. But I wanted to buy her drinks. I wanted to know her more than anything in my whole life.

The waiter asked me if I would like anything from the trolley. I looked up; my throat was dry and I ordered an americano with cream in a husky voice, clearing it as the words were coming out. I caught her glancing over as I ordered. I saw the sun was shining through my window onto her face. Her eyes sparkled like diamonds, multi-coloured like rainbows.

As the waiter passed my drink, I failed to hold it properly, spilling it as I rested it on my table. I was no longer in control of my own body; I had been taken over by emotions. I was no longer the confident outgoing person I once was. I turned my head back to looking out the window and saw the sign to Paris that said "225km". I knew there would only be ninety minutes left of the journey. I panicked. I had to get to know her in ninety minutes or lose her forever.

I was observing her drinking her coffee. Her deep red lipstick had left a kiss on the cup. I was becoming infatuated with a woman I hardly knew who was taking over all my emotions usually reserved for somebody in a long-term relationship. Everything she did got my attention. I had to move up a step or move on. I started to settle into my seat from the edge to a more comfortable position. I turned to look outside the window and felt a tap on my shoulder.

There she stood: my dream girl.

"Can you look after my bag and coat please? Whilst I go to the bathroom."

Clearing my voice, I replied, "Of course."

I made it my job to look after her possessions as if there was anything missing it would not go down well. It was a long time before she came back but apologised for being so long. She said it was due to not travelling well on trains. She had a phobia of them. She had opened the windows between carriages and had some fresh air.

She sat down and introduced herself, "I'm Jasmin."

"Hello, Jasmin. I'm Mateo."

"That is a nice name. What does it mean?"

"A gift from God," I replied.

"I am impressed," Jasmin said.

"Thank you. It was my late father's name. He was Italian and my mother was English. I spent twenty years in New York growing up so you could say I was more American than Italian or English. Although my passion runs with my Italian side after my father."

"You are a very handsome man, Mateo. Do you look like your father? Your eyes are very dark and mysterious."

"Well, I am not sure, Jasmin, whether they have any mystery behind them. My father married only one woman: my mother. And they were in love until he passed away."

"What do you do for a living, Mateo?"

"That is a big question, Jasmin. I am a financial wizard."

"Does that mean you do spells?"

"No, of course not. It means I make people money out of nothing."

"Wow, that's good, Mateo. Are you sure you cannot make me disappear?"

"Not you, Jasmin. I have only just begun to know you. I do not want you to disappear now but I would like to disappear into those beautiful eyes of yours."

"You are too kind," Jasmin replied. "Have you any plans when you get to Paris? Are you there to meet someone?"

"No, Jasmin. I am here as I have a broken relationship of six years behind me. I suppose I am running away as I thought we would be together forever. How about you, Jasmin?"

"Well, I do not know where to start. I am a widow; my husband was a motorcycle racer and was killed recently in a bad accident on the track. He was leading the race when it started to rain and there was a big crash, and he only survived a short while before he passed away."

"That is not good, Jasmin. I am so sorry for your loss."

"He knew the risks," Jasmin replied, "But it was his passion, and it took his life. I am so sad, but I must move on with my life."

"So, what are you doing in Paris, Jasmin?"

"I have never been, and I promised to go one day. So, I thought now was a suitable time to see one of the places on my bucket list."

"Well done, Jasmin. I am glad you came on this trip to hopefully put him to rest and enjoy your life. Would you meet me in Paris for a drink?"

"Yes, I am sure we can meet. I would like that. We seem to be in the same predicament. We are both running away from our past relationships. I am not sure I will ever find anybody like him again. Give me your number and I will ring you and arrange something."

"We could go to Paris together. I know a charming hotel near the Eiffel Tower. Would you spend some time with me? We might be good for each other, Jasmin."

"Mateo, I was going to stay with a friend but cannot reach her so I could probably spend a couple of days with you."

"Okay, it would be nice to have your company, Jasmin. I am glad you accepted. I know a lovely restaurant close to the Eiffel Tower. It has a magic feel to it and the food is to die for."

"That sounds great, Mateo. I cannot wait. What about the hotel? Can we go there and get freshened up? I am happy if it's a platonic relationship. I'm not sleeping with you?"

"No, Jasmin. I would never try on anything like that. I am happy just being with you and enjoying your company."

The train pulled into the station and we made our way to the hotel reception.

"Jasmin, it's room 242, second floor. Would you like to go to the room and change ready for tonight and I will do the check in?"

I entered the room.

"My God, Jasmin, you look beautiful. Let's go out to the restaurant. I have booked it so we are good to go."

Jasmin linked arms with me and said, "Me and my handsome man off on our adventure."

"It's just up the road from here, Jasmin."

It was turning cold outside, but my body was glowing. I had the woman of my dreams on my arm. I loved it.

Chapter 2

Mateo

"Good evening, Mateo. Would you like your usual table?" said the waiter.

"What is happening here, Mateo?" Jasmin said in a questionable voice.

"Do not worry, Jasmin. I used to have to come to Paris two times a month for work. This is how I came to know this place. It was always business, not pleasure."

"I forgive you then. Can we have a drink first please, Mateo? Before dinner," she asked.

"Yes, of course. Let us sit down and look at the menu."

Jasmin said, "This place has a lovely ambiance to it. I love all the crystal and water fountains. It has a tranquil setting. I feel so comfortable here with you."

While ordering the wine, I found myself looking across the table staring into her eyes. They took me to a place I had never been. It was like looking into a dark sky lit by stars from a faraway galaxy. I felt like I was floating on the edge of another world. I hoped I would never come down.

The meal arrived and it was impeccable as usual.

As we left the restaurant, we turned the corner to see the Eiffel Tower lit up in all its glory. Jasmin threw her arms around my shoulders, kissing me on the cheek and thanking me for being me and looking after her. I felt a new emotion of protection for this newfound love as I put my arm around her waist. I felt myself going into a semi-conscious state. If this was love, I needed more. It felt like I was floating in a surreal place where everything was beautiful.

We walked around chatting and laughing about times in our lives we remembered as being funny and memorable while growing up. We were becoming so close, and I loved every minute of it.

We arrived back at the hotel and Jasmin said she had really enjoyed the night, but she was tired and ready for bed. She asked if she could use the bathroom first. I said, of course. I went and sat on the bed scrolling through the television for something to watch. As I looked across to the bathroom, the door was slightly open. I saw her evening dress on the floor and Jasmin walked across the bathroom in red underwear. She looked stunning but sexy at the same time. This lady was beautiful. I wanted her to be mine forever. I could never see myself with anybody else. I was in love.

The bathroom door opened and Jasmin came into the bedroom wearing a baby doll style top. She was fairly tall; her legs seemed to go on forever. She was something else. I could see she had the body of a goddess like she had been made perfectly in a factory. Jasmin said goodnight and got into bed. Lying on her back, her silk-like hair flowed over the pillow.

I spent no time getting out of the bathroom into the bedroom to be next to her. We wished each other goodnight and we turned back-to-back. It seemed like forever but then we both turned to each other. I could see her as the light from the road lit the room. She stared into my eyes and smiled; her teeth were so white they looked like pearls out of an exotic ocean. I had never seen teeth so perfect. What a woman.

She moved towards me and put my arms around her. The next thing I knew, it was morning.

Chapter 3

Mateo

As I woke up, she was looking at me and leant over and kissed me on my lips. The kiss was something else; so sweet and moist, it made my senses go into overtime.

She asked if I would be taking her anywhere and I said it was a secret as to where we were going. We went downstairs to have breakfast. We laughed as she tried to find out where we were going as we left the hotel. We took a different direction to last night, but it bought us back to the same place.

As we turned the corner, the Eiffel Tower was there.

"That's where we are going," I said.

She tightened her grip on my hand.

"Yes," I added, "Right to the top."

"I am scared of heights."

"Don't worry, you are with me. I will look after you."

She kissed me on the cheek and said, "Thank you, my darling."

It was busy and we joined the queue.

"How long will it take us to get to the top?" she asked.

"We will take the stairs, so it will take around forty-five minutes in between stopping to look around. You will be able to see how the city has been made to look like a round cake. With the Eiffel Tower being the centre and all the avenues are between the slices with all the fabulous buildings fronting them."

It was a long way up and Jasmin cried out, laughing.

I said, "There is a long way to go yet."

But we both agreed it was good exercise and carried on climbing to the next level. What a long way it seemed, but I had done it all before. To a newcomer, it was a trek to the top.

As we reached the middle section before the main tower, I carried Jasmin the last fifty steps with her arms tightly wrapped around my shoulders.

"Don't drop me," she said in a quiet voice so as not to bring too much attention to us. I would have carried her three hundred steps. She was now my woman enjoying every minute of every step.

As we came out of the stairway, I put her down. She hugged and kissed me and thanked me for helping her. I said she was welcome, and I took her hand and walked to the edge to feast her eyes at the sight of the city. We had a drink of hot chocolate in the restaurant before going to the top of the tower. I kidded her that we were going to have to go up as many steps again.

She gasped, "No. Can we stay here?"

I laughed and said, "Come on, we will take the lift to the top."

As we got to the summit of the tower, looking over the people below looked really small. Jasmin held me round the waist in a tight grip.

"I am not letting go," she said. As we looked around the city trying to identify different areas, she added, "I feel safe holding onto you."

It made me smile and she reached up and kissed my cheek, as we rounded the end of the circle. It was so nice. We started to make our way down after a photo shoot at the summit. Jasmin was excited she had been right to the top of the Eiffel Tower. Nothing was going to stop her from being an explorer now.

"I want you to take me everywhere, Mateo."

We spent the rest of the day walking down the Champs-Élysées looking through the shops. We found a really nice restaurant and sat out in the autumn sun under the boulevard marquee. The place was busy. We had to wait for a table, but the food and wine were excellent.

As we sat there, drinking good wine and people watching, passers-by came in their droves. We sat relaxing after the day.

It was getting dark and a bit cooler. We were not dressed for the cold night, so we decided to go back to the hotel for the last night. Tomorrow, we were going to travel down to the city of Leon.

We got to the bedroom and Jasmin threw her arms around me and kissed me for what seemed to be a really long time. I felt I was going to have to come up for air. She told me she was falling for me, and she loved my company and everything about me. I was shocked but glad we were more than just friends now. Not lovers yet but I hoped soon as I wanted her so bad. She aroused all my senses. I needed to get in a cold shower and cool down.

Jasmin went into the bathroom and whilst I was looking outside onto the boulevard, she walked across behind me and put her arms around me. She squeezed me and told me she loved me.

I turned around and looked at my woman and said, "I love you more."

She was wearing only a bra and panties. How beautiful she looked. I hugged her, trying to make sure my hands were not going anywhere but around her shoulders, although my mind was running wild.

I was in a passionate embrace with a beautiful woman half naked in a hotel room in Paris. How could it get any better than this? I thought I had died and gone to heaven. I wanted her so bad, but I decided I was in control of my emotions and I would wait until she was ready. I would not make any suggestive moves.

We got into bed, and she lay over me and held me tight, kissing me. I was the luckiest man in the world. She must have known I was excited as it was evident. She smiled as if she knew but I did not want to rush in and spoil anything. We fell asleep and I woke up to feel her stroking the skin on my face looking into my eyes as I opened them fully. She told me I had beautiful skin and that she loved me so much. I was glad I had not taken advantage of her the night before. We were both in love. I wanted it to be perfect and make sure my intentions were honourable.

Chapter 4

Mateo

After breakfast, we got the bus to Leon. We talked and laughed our heads off all the way down nearly. It was a long journey, but we got there together. That's all that mattered to me.

Walking along by the side of the city motorway, we could see the prison. The prisoners were shouting, "Je t'aime."

"Je t'aime? What does that mean?" Jasmin asked.

"They are saying they love you," I replied.

"Wow," she said, "How do I tell them I love them back?"

I was impressed she wanted to say anything back.

"It's 'je t'aime aussi'. It means 'I love you too'."

She kissed me and shouted, "Je t'aime aussi."

The prisoners were in an uproar, shouting, "Belle, belle."

"That's beautiful," I told her.

"I want to learn French so I can speak and reply to all the French people. I love it here."

As we were walking, we saw houseboats to rent.

"Let's do it," I said.

"Yes, it will be great going down the river," Jasmin replied.

We hired the houseboat and after instructions we made our way down the river. It was still hot with no sign of cold weather. We had moved six hundred and forty kilometres south of Paris. It seemed everything had come to life. Dragonflies were dancing off the water catching small flies and mosquitoes. The fish were surfacing to catch them as well. Everything seemed like they were mating. Thoughts came into my head as Jasmin dangled her legs over the side of the boat, thinking when it would be our turn.

All at once, whilst leaning forwards, Jasmin fell into the river. The river was large and deep, and the current was fast. I could see her being swept away. I cut the engine and dived into the water. It was cold and all I could see was the love of my life being swept away. She was struggling to keep her head above water and she kept on going under. The current was too strong for her.

I was swimming fast to catch her up. As I got closer, I saw her go under the water. I dived under and could just see her disappearing. I had to act fast, or I would lose her to the river. I swam like my life depended on it.

Just as the river rounded the bend, I saw her head out the water again. I did a fast crawl swim and just managed to catch her before the river started to go to rapids. I only just got her in time and pulled her to the riverbank. The banks were so high, and I did not want to lose her here, so I swam with her head above the water further down the stream where I managed to get her out. She was in shock, and she needed medical help.

Other boat owners had seen what had happened and emergency services were on the way. I had been trained in CPR, and I began to administer it to her. She spluttered and water came out of her mouth. She was alive but cold. She was hypothermic and needed keeping warm. I was rubbing her body to warm her up.

"Has anybody got a blanket or coat to keep her warm?" I shouted.

Jasmin was fairly lifeless. I checked her breathing. It was fine, but we had to get her to hospital fast before the cold killed her. We waited ten minutes for the ambulance to come but it seemed like hours at the time. They put her on a stretcher, and I held her hand in the ambulance to the hospital. They said she was in a bad way but stable. I was relieved she would be okay, and I would have the love of my life back soon.

Jasmin was in hospital for two days and when I went to collect her, she ran towards me and literally threw herself

29

around me kissing me and not letting go. We went back to the houseboat to collect our belongings but never went on it again. She thanked me for saving her life as she now had so much to live for. I was just so happy to see her alive and thinking of how it could have turned out if I was not a good swimmer. Those days at the swimming baths and swimming in the quarries had paid off.

Chapter 5

Mateo

We decided between us to head off to St Tropez for some chill time after Leon. My love was now well, and it was all behind us. We had everything to look forward to; discovering the south of France together.

We booked into a small hotel in the centre of St Tropez. Jasmin, although telling me she loved me, was struggling to get back to the girl I fell in love with. She never left my side all the way down to not wanting me out of her sight. She was glowing and looked absolutely gorgeous in her small denim shorts and black vest. She had caught the sun and her skin looked sun-kissed. She had painted her toenails in white varnish to match her fingernails. They looked elegant; her fingers were long and slender which made them complement the varnish.

We left our bags and went for a walk along the beach. It was just nice: not too hot, but warm. Jasmin was enjoying walking in the wet sand looking for shells and rocks. I could see she was opening up again and nearly back to her old self. As I looked at her, my heart melted. Maybe this was our time to enjoy life. We had all the ingredients for it: sun, sand, a beautiful woman and time. I was going to make sure this worked as we were both so happy. I told Jasmin I had a sister that lived in Tuscany in Italy and that I would like to go there and visit her if she could spare the time.

"Mateo, I would love to go. I want to go everywhere with you. I love you."

A smile came over my face. This was the woman for me. I was so proud to be her man.

We walked miles along the beach and rocks discovering small coves and beaches. We sat on a private beach. Nobody was around and we kissed and held each other. We were so happy to be here. It was nearly dusk and the sky was getting dark, so we started to make our way back to the harbour. We found a beautiful restaurant overlooking the harbour. It was all lit up like a postcard. We sat there and had a fish meal and drank wine looking at the starlit sky. How beautiful it was. I told Jasmin I could not decide who was the most beautiful: the stars or her.

"You win every time, my love," I said when she looked at me.

She told me she loved me, and she had been waiting all her life for someone like me. Although she loved her husband, the love was not the same as the love for me. Her husband's true love was motorbike racing and not her.

I moved my seat next to her and put my arm around her, kissing her gently on the lips. I could taste her. She was beautiful. Maybe this was all a big plan the lord had for us: to meet in this way and to fall in love. Or was it a chance meeting on a train? Whichever it was, I was happy and appreciated the time together.

It was warm still in the square and we sat out until 11pm. The stars were still shining as we went back to the hotel. We were in another world; everything was perfect. We were still to make love but this, although the right place, was not the right time. We went to bed wrapped around each other. It was so nice. It was love.

Chapter 6

Mateo

The next day, we looked around the shops and on the square after breakfast. The sun was starting to get hot. Jasmin looked fabulous as normal in yellow skirt-like shorts; her long legs and sandals co-ordinated with her red cropped top. Her midriff was showing her toned body. She looked sexy and was getting attention everywhere. She was a real head-turner. I was beginning to feel jealous but did not show it. She was mine and nobody else's.

She put her arm through mine, kissed me and showed them all who she loved. My jealously dissipated into love for her. She was stunning and absolutely lovely; a one-man woman. Nobody was taking her away from me no matter how much money they had or how good-looking they were. Jasmin was like a flower. She was in full bloom and looked stunning. We were looking in a shop and she tried a small leather bracelet on. It was five euros and she wanted it to remind her of this day in St Tropez.

We sat down and I ordered a bottle of wine. It was a Châteauneuf-du-Pape 1998. Jasmin tested the wine and approved the bottle. I could taste it on her lips as I kissed her. She loved it and got off her chair and kissed me back in front of the whole restaurant. People were clapping and admiring her. I must say I was slightly embarrassed, but she was the most beautiful girl in the south of France, and I was lucky to have her. I was going to enjoy every moment I could with her.

As we finished the bottle of wine, a couple asked if we wanted to join them as they were English and they could tell we spoke English too. We said we would be delighted to join them. We all introduced ourselves and ordered more wine.

Our new friends were Michael and Jane. They were on holiday like us. They said they had sailed in from Majorca, Spain. We got talking about all things topical, including their boat. They had a forty-four foot catamaran in the harbour, which they invited us to look at. They said it was a brand new one this year. They used to have a forty foot one and this one was slightly bigger.

As we got onto the boat, it began to rock. I could see Jasmin was nervous and did not feel safe. I told her it would be okay and if we went out, she would have to wear a life jacket.

We started to pull out the harbour and we cleared it soon to open sea and found ourselves offshore. The sails went up as they had electric winches and we felt the wind take the boat very fast. It was exciting but also scary as one side of the boat was out of the water. They said it was normal but we wondered if we should have gone on. Jasmin seemed to settle down and started to enjoy the sailing. After all, it was a fabulous boat. We headed towards St Raphael. It was choppy out at sea, but the catamaran was more than capable of taking it. I had some knowledge of sailing, so I helped out whilst Jasmin lay on the deck chilling out enjoying the ride. She looked stunning, like she belonged there. I think she had a presence about her where people wanted to be around her; she made them look good and interesting.

We rounded outside the port and headed back to St Tropez. We had six dolphins shadowing the boat, jumping out of the water like they were showing off. It was lovely to see them. Jasmin was infatuated by them and said she would love to swim with them.

I said, "You have done enough swimming on this holiday."

She laughed and carried on looking at the display the dolphins were giving. She blew me a kiss across the boat and made a love heart sign with her hands. She was so nice. The lifestyle suited her.

Michael and Jane were pleased to have us both on board. I got on with Michael, and Jane and Jasmin looked like they had been friends for life.

As we got off the boat in the harbour, Michael said they had to be back in Majorca for Monday so they would be leaving in the morning, but they would love for us to join them in Majorca soon. We had made some nice friends and I hoped to catch up later with them.

All good things come to an end, and it was time for us to move on from St Tropez. I think Jasmin would have liked to stay but there were no more rooms available, and we had to be out tomorrow after breakfast. Jasmin seemed to be a lot better and really enjoyed the time and the sun. I felt we were just friends now, but I was hoping it was just leading her back to love me as she did in Paris. I was prepared to wait for as long as it took.

Next stop: Cannes.

Chapter 7

Mateo

We are here at last in Cannes.

"Mateo, where are we staying?" Jasmin asked.

"Well, my love, I have found us a nice hotel on the promenade facing the sea," I said and we went to the room.

Jasmin said, "You know I love you, Mateo. More than you could ever know. I loved you the first night we spent together in Paris. It's a wonderful city for romance. I wanted you to take me and make love to me, but you seemed distant and restrained."

"Jasmin, I am sorry. I thought you were in mourning for your husband, and I did not want to upset you by making any moves on you."

Jasmin leant over and kissed me on the cheek.

"You are a wonderful handsome man who I adore and love unconditionally. Give me a second to get into something more comfortable."

I waited as I also wanted to use the bathroom. It had been a hot transfer from St Tropez. At that moment, Jasmin came out wearing only her black silk underwear.

"Take me, Mateo, take me now."

I exploded with emotion; tears appeared in my eyes. It was not what I expected as I was waiting for her and all the time, she was mine for the taking. I was so in love with her, it hurt to ever think about being only friends and not lovers. This was my time to secure the woman of my life. I had to take it slow and show her love and not rush in and spoil the moment. She was a dream woman and she belonged to me. I wanted to explore her beauty and lavish every moment. How lucky I was. I thought about the moment we first spoke on the train. Now I could take the woman of my dreams to bed and make beautiful love to her. I said to myself, there is a god after all. God bless.

Next morning, after breakfast and a beautiful night of love and passion, we decided to have a look around Cannes.

"I would like my photo taken on the steps of the Cannes film festival with my man."

"Of course. What a lovely picture that will be," I replied.

We managed to find somebody and gave them our phones to take the picture. Jasmin was really happy to have the photo. She seemed to be buzzing all day about it and kept looking at it. She was so happy. The place was beautiful and so was Jasmin. I was having to pinch myself. Were we actually here in this fabulous place?

We looked around the harbour. We were having a competition identifying whose yacht was worth the most money. Jasmin was looking at one and the steward asked if we would like to come on board and have a look around it.

"Wow," said Jasmin, "How the other half live. I would like a yacht here in paradise. To wake up here every day."

It was really hot and we decided to walk along the promenade where there was a coolness from the sea. The wind was gently blowing. I could see her hair moving across her chest dancing over her breasts. She looked ravishing as we chattered.

We passed the Carlton Intercontinental Hotel.

Jasmin said, "Can we go into the hotel and look around? It looks fabulous."

We walked up the front path to the foyer where the door man asked if we were guests.

"No," I replied, "But we are meeting somebody here that is a guest."

We were allowed in and we looked around. I said to Jasmin the next time we were in Cannes, we would stay here. Coming out of the hotel, we turned left.

I said to Jasmin, "There is a restaurant here on the corner of the road. It has outdoor seating."

It was too nice to pass by, so we sat down and ordered a bottle of wine.

"Bonjour," I said to the waiter.

"Bonjour," the waiter replied and smiled at Jasmin, "Tu es magnifique, mademoiselle."

Jasmin smiled.

I said, "Merci, monsieur."

And he left.

Jasmin said, "What did he say?"

I replied, "He said you looked wonderful."

She was radiant in the sun and seemed really happy. The waiter bought over some complimentary olives and bread. It was such a beautiful day. Jasmin was looking over to the sea and asked if the cordoned off areas were private beaches.

"Yes," I said, "They belong to the Martinez Hotel across the road and the Carlton Intercontinental."

"I would spend my whole day there if I could but we are having fun here. We do not need a private beach," said Jasmin.

We had our own share of views here. We ordered a second bottle of wine. The waiter seemed to look at Jasmin like he wanted to make her his, she was so attractive. He bought us more canapés as I think he just wanted to have contact with us. He would top up our wine like we were celebrities. Watching us to see when we were ready for more wine in our glasses.

I noticed two men coming out of the Martinez Hotel. They seemed to look over at us then walked past the restaurant. Jasmin was looking at them as they were over-dressed for the day. They went by and I saw them sit down at the table behind us at the rear of the restaurant. I felt they were looking at us but put it down to Jasmin attracting them with her stunning looks. Everyone was looking at her.

We asked for the bill and made our way back to the sea front and walked towards the boat jetty. It was a long walk there and we managed to get a drink and an ice cream from a surf type shack on the promenade. We climbed over the sea wall and lay on the beach, looking up at the stars in the dark sky. The sand was white and soft.

Her hand gently touched mine and she squeezed it.

"You are the best thing that ever happened to me," Jasmin said.

I felt her leg cross over mine. They were as soft as the sand we were lying on. She started to rub my leg with hers around my calf. I could feel a tingle right up to my ears. What a sensual feeling this was knowing we were a couple again. Jasmin put her hand on my upper leg and started to move up. I was no longer transfixed by the stars. There was one shining brighter next to me. She was hot and wanted me.

I pulled her on top of me. I felt her legs spread out over me. She gently grabbed my wrists with her hands and moved my arms above my head in a kind of submissive gesture. I felt her hot body caressing mine. Jasmin had her senses firing on all cylinders. If we were cars, we were out for the ride of our lives.

Despite the fact we were on a public beach and would be safer looking at the stars, we were nearly there and had to restrain ourselves from going to the exciting stage.

Jasmin said, "Let's go for it." Jasmin had become daring and exciting.

I said in a quiet voice, "We would not go down well with the Cannes tabloids."

We both laughed and I held her hand. True love was a great gift. It only came on a rare occasion and for some people it never came at all. But we had both found it and we were going to milk it to the max. We sat there listening to the waves gently lapping at the shore; the stars lighting up the dark sky.

"Can it get any better than this?" I whispered to Jasmin, "Are we in heaven?"

We made our way off the beach back to the hotel. It was late. Jasmin ran in the corridor towards the door.

"Come on, run faster. I need you, Mateo," she shouted.

I moved from a fast walk to a rapid run. As the door opened, Jasmin rushed in and started removing her clothes as she ran towards the bed. She was that hot she was melting.

"Mateo," she shouted. Her clothes seemed to just drop off her, revealing her fabulous body. I had never been so lucky as to see somebody so ravishing as her.

Jasmin lay there stroking her breasts. They just stood to attention. I was so excited that she was there for me. This woman was on fire. As I jumped on the bed, Jasmin caught me, squeezing my torso. She wanted me so bad. How was I going to satisfy her insatiable appetite for love? She wanted to make love. I knew I was in for the long haul, but she was like a grid map and I wanted to discover every centimetre of her body. We were nude in a passionate embrace. I was not going for gold. I wanted this to last all night. I wanted it to be her night and enjoy every moment. We kissed and made love so many times; neither of us kept count.

As she fell asleep, the dawn sun was shining through the gaps in the curtains. Jasmin lay on her front. I could see her curves lit up by the rays from the sun. I just wanted to watch her sleep. What a night. I lay at the side of her and wrapped around her, and she stirred.

"Thank you, darling. You are the best," she said gently.

I felt myself drifting off to sleep. I started to wake up, but I felt like I had never been to sleep, to see Jasmin making a drink of tea. She noticed I had woken up.

"Would you like a drink?" she asked. She was dressed only in her underwear.

I was more interested in looking at her as she moved around the room while bringing my cup to the bed. She leant over to give it to me. *What a woman*, I thought as I looked at her body. It was perfect from her head to her toes; she was everything rolled into one. I pulled her arm and she fell onto the bed and we made love again. This was love, not sex. Sex was only a moment of relief. This was full on love and I was excited.

Chapter 8

Mateo

Soon, it was time to leave Cannes and the next stop on our journey was Antibes. We caught the scenic bus there. It was a really nice trip along the south shore. The sea looked like a shade of light blue, and you could see the sun shimmering over the surface only broken by the crashing waves on the beach. The rocks seemed to poke out of the sea like they were waiting to be fed. The whole scenery was captivating and seemed like it was trying to pull us in closer. We were laughing and joking and enjoying the trip. Jasmin had not let go of my hand all the way there.

She had been very attentive. She had thanked me for bringing her with me to these beautiful places. She was loving it all as the bus pulled alongside of the harbour.

"Look, Mateo," she said, "Look at all the lovely sailing yachts. There are lots of them. Can we see them later?"

"Yes, Jasmin. We will see them later."

As we got into the hotel, Jasmin whispered, "I am really horny. Can we make love when we get into the room?"

"Jasmin, are you trying to kill me? You want to make love again?"

"Yes," Jasmin said, "I want you to love me exactly the same as last night. I have been thinking about last night all day. I need you more than you can imagine. I love you."

"I love you more, Jasmin," I replied.

As we got to our room, the door was slightly open. We walked inside and some of the cupboard doors were open and the drawers were not fully closed either.

"This is strange. They have not finished off the room," I said. However, it seemed clean and ready for use. "I am having a shower, baby, as I feel tired and I want to wake up."

I took off my clothes and turned on the shower. The water was hot and started steaming up the shower cubical. As I washed my face, the door opened and Jasmin was there, naked.

"Can I join you, my darling?" she asked, touching me in a sensitive place. "You are a big boy."

She stepped into the shower and began to kiss me passionately. What a woman. What a beautiful person Jasmin was.

My hands were all over her. She was excited and showed it. I was behind her with my hands on her front moving to all her sensual places. She had her head turned, kissing me.

"Mateo, you are the best," she shouted.

I was fearful the room next door would report us. It was getting hot and noisy. Jasmin was hotter than the sun. I shower jetted her all over and made sure she was really satisfied with the service I was giving her. She said she had never been made love to with anyone like me.

"I feel my whole body is a temple and you're worshipping it. Every day, it's better than the day before," she added.

I dried her body. I could feel every curve as the towel rubbed down her silky skin. I wanted her but not in the shower. I wanted to make love to this sensual woman. I wanted her in the bed. I pulled her towards me; my skin still wet. I had no time to dry myself. I had to get her into bed. I was boiling over with emotion. We made love and made love again. She wanted me so bad. We lay in bed wrapped that tightly together you would not be able to get a knife between us.

"Jasmin, are you asleep?"

"No, Mateo. I am just enjoying the moment. You went so deep, Mateo. I can still feel you now. I love you. I love you."

"I love you more," I replied. "Let's go out. It's getting late."

As I was locking the door, Jasmin put her arm in mine, her head on my shoulder and kissed my neck. It was so nice to be so close. We were about a five-minute walk away from the main square. I said we should find a nice place to eat there. Jasmin looked amazing as usual. I was the cock of the walk strutting down the street hand in hand with the south of France's finest. I looked at her and she smiled. She was so happy, it made me have goose pimples all over to think I could make her this happy.

We found a nice bistro behind the harbour walls. It felt really warm still for the time of year.

"Pick the table, Jasmin," I said.

She picked one at the rear of the forecourt saying she wanted to sit there so she could see everybody and people watch all night. We had a steak each: a fillet. It tasted so good; it just melted in your mouth. Our tongues were dancing with the taste of it.

Later, a trio band came on to the patio. They were good and the music was chilled. Jasmin and I danced the night away, never out of each other's arms. Jasmin could dance well. I came out of a twirl with her and let her go and she danced back. She was the centre of attention. Everyone was looking. *Someone up there was taking care of me*, I thought.

The night finished and we walked back to the hotel. Just before the hotel, there was an entertainer with a dog. The dog was so talented, so we stayed and watched the show. Jasmin seemed a little on edge and was looking around. I asked if she was okay.

"Yes, darling, thank you," she replied and asked me for a hug. I gave her the biggest one I could. She told me not to let go, that she was loving it so much and she felt safe in my arms. We walked into the hotel, kissed and went to bed.

"Tomorrow is another day," she said. She could not wait.

I woke up to find Jasmin spread eagled over me with nothing on but her smile. She was perfect all over apart from a long scar on the top of her arm. It looked so straight but not new. She had probably had an accident with something sharp.

Chapter 9

Mateo

The next day, we skipped breakfast as we lay in and missed the time slot. I said we should find a nice bakery and have a baguette or something and a coffee. We walked around looking.

"That looks nice over there," said Jasmin.

We found a seat and sat down.

"Bonjour," I said to the counter staff member.

"Bonjour," she replied.

"Three croissants and two large expressos please, mademoiselle."

Jasmin came over and took the croissants and I carried the coffees. As she got close, I could smell her sweet scent. She had put her perfume on, and it smelled amazing. It was nearly as beautiful as her.

We sat down and enjoyed the fresh baked food. I had bought some additional cakes and they tasted really good and fresh. They were made in ovens on the premises; this was a quality bakery. I looked outside in the yard and I saw four men. Two looked like the men I had seen the day before. It was strange they were here too. Was it just a coincidence? I kept it to myself so as not to alarm Jasmin too much. I turned my back as if I had not seen them. We drank our coffee and left. I looked back I could see they were looking over our way. *What were they doing there?* I thought.

We walked down to the harbour. I was concerned but did not show it to Jasmin. She was just enjoying the walk, humming a tune from a record skipping as she walked. I kept taking a quick look round to ensure we were not being followed. I was still keeping my eye out for them as surely this could not be another coincidence. Why now was there four men? A strange combination, all of them looking out of place in Antibes. What was their motive for being here? Were they working on some project? *Maybe*, I thought, *they could be on holiday as friends*. I cast it aside in my mind and put my attention back on Jasmin who was in another world taking in the beauty of Antibes.

We went to the market and there was an auction of jewellery. Not of good quality but one piece took her eye.

"Bid on it for me, Mateo," she said in a hurried voice.

I looked at my money. We had enough to go in for the bid. We actually bid last and ended up buying a ring.

"Yes, yes," she shouted, jumping in the air like a young teenager. I was not embarrassed this was my woman.

After paying for the ring, Jasmin was quiet whilst she tried it on. She moved it from one finger to another. Was it going to fit her wedding ring finger? She tried desperately to put it on the third finger of her left hand but it would only fit on the other hand.

"We are still married. I don't want you looking like you are free. You are taken now. You are mine, Mateo."

I was happy to go along with whatever she said. It made her happy and that made me happy. We continued walking into the area of the harbour where the yachts were.

"Can we have one of these? I would love to go out on one," she asked. She appeared to have a love for boats but hated the water. It's usually people that love boats, love the water too. Probably she had a bad experience before Leon and Leon did not help. We looked around and managed to go down the boardwalk and speak to a boat owner that said he had been out a few hours but the sea was turning rough so he made it back in haste.

"It's good to know you are safe," I said and we wished him a good day.

We started to walk around the top of the harbour, and we stopped to look at all the sailing ships racing. They looked splendid. We sat watching them, holding each other for what seemed like hours. Where was the time going? It flew by every day.

We walked through the main square. It was so vibrant. Everybody was busy doing something. It felt good and it made us enjoy the day even more. Jasmin was looking at a store trying on hats. I pretended to walk on as if I had not seen her go in.

"Mateo," she cried as I carried on walking. She ran towards me and jumped on my back, kissing me when she got down. "That was not funny."

I laughed and said, "You are always in my sight, Jasmin."

She smiled and asked me to stay with her always. She seemed really concerned that I should not walk off on my own. Was it just a jealous moment or was it a woman's intuition? I grabbed her hand and started walking. We stopped for a drink outside in a courtyard where they had some parrots hanging up in cages. They were funny as they spoke different languages. Bonjour was the favourite, but there was also Anglais.

"That is French for English," I told her.

The parrot said, "Bonjour, mademoiselle."

Jasmin laughed and said she had never heard a parrot speak French before. We were enjoying the moment and Jasmin asked if she could go to the shop as she wanted to buy me something special.

"Yes, of course," I said, "Just be careful."

She was gone close to an hour, but when she came back, she apologised for going for so long. She said she wanted something really memorable for me but could not find what she wanted. We sat down and had some food.

We talked about what we liked to do in our spare time between work. It was funny as mine was always about being away from the office, where Jasmin's was always action-packed. She loved sky diving out of aeroplanes at high altitude and she told me how she could join a circle in the air. I was inquisitive.

"What actually got you into sky diving?" I asked her.

"It's a long story," she said, "I have a lot of friends that do it. We all get a buzz out of it."

Wow, I thought. I was not sure it was my kind of relaxation away from work. She said she loved everything outdoors. Any sport, flying, power boat racing, hand gliding, parachuting... the list went on. She loved it all.

We finished our drinks and started to walk back to the hotel. It was hot walking back; we were ready for a nice rest.

As we got to the hotel room, Jasmin kicked off her sandals.

"I am really tired," she said. She looked like she had been on a long walk and had not cooled down from her shopping trip. She collapsed on the bed and was asleep in minutes. I went to move her handbag onto the dressing tabletop. It felt heavy. I put it down and the clasp opened.

As I was closing it, I noticed there was a gun inside. What? Where had this come from? Who was this lady?

Why did she have a gun? I looked over. She was out of it with the wine and the long walk; it had taken its toll on her. I was inquisitive as I had never seen a real gun before. I went to the bathroom for some toilet tissue. I did not want my fingerprints on it. I carefully wrapped the tissue around the barrel of the gun and lifted it out of the bag. It was bright chrome in colour with an inlaid pearl handle. I was scared. What was she doing with this? It looked real to me.

I placed it on the tabletop and looked further into the handbag. I had to know who this woman was. My world was upside down. As I felt around the bag, there were two steel bullet magazines. I could see the bullets showing out the top of them. I left them in the bag and put the gun back and closed the bag. As the clasp closed, it clicked and made a noise.

I looked over at Jasmin. She looked up fast; it had disturbed her. Luckily, I had moved away. She looked at me and the bag and closed her eyes. I was really scared. I found myself questioning my own thoughts on who she could be and why she was here with me. I would have to try to sleep it off.

Jasmin woke up and put her arms out. She said she wanted me to come and hug her. It was a strange moment holding her. Was this my Jasmin?

"Come to bed, darling," she said.

I said I had a headache. I just was not feeling it, although she still melted my heart to look at her. She was not the Jasmin I knew earlier today.

I had to make some moves to find out about her. What she was up to and why? Jasmin was so lovely in every way. What was she caught up in? Was somebody chasing or threatening her? I needed to know. Maybe I could help her with whatever she was mixed up in. I would have to help her. After all, this was my woman and I needed to protect her. I felt I was out of my depth.

In for a penny, in for a pound, I thought. I was going for it. I just had to find the right time to discuss the problems she was having. The love we had could not be fake. It had to be genuine. I searched my soul for an answer.

Chapter 10

Mateo

As we left the hotel, there was a man outside in the street. He looked away as we walked along the pavement. He was looking down, but I felt he was waiting for us. What was going on? Why were we being followed? Jasmin did not seem stirred by him.

"Come on. Let's go to the marina," she said.

As I turned round, he had gone.

We had a leisurely walk down the jetty. We had a look around at the boats coming into the harbour. It was a nice day; a bit clammy but bearable.

Walking back, we saw the man again. He was walking towards us; I could see he was reaching under his coat.

Jasmin looked and said, "Run."

We started to run back to where we had come from. He was running fast and catching up. He was just about caught up when Jasmin stopped abruptly turning round and sweeping his legs from underneath him in a sliding tackle. He went down and hit the ground hard. Spinning around, Jasmin, in a split second, hit the front of his neck with a karate chop. She got up but he was in a bad way.

I saw her lift up his head and snap his neck.

Under her breath, she said, "You won't be bothering us again." She dragged him to the side of the jetty and threw him in the harbour. "Fish bait."

I was shocked. It was so fast. It was like it never happened. We were responsible for a man's death. Between us, we had killed him.

Jasmin picked up her bag and said, "Let's go, before he is missed."

We hurried along the jetty and made our way back to the square. We didn't speak all the way back to the hotel. As we got in, I asked Jasmin what he was after.

Jasmin replied, "He was after you."

I was shocked, "Why was he after me? And who was he?"

"His name was Epiect Susset. A freelance mercenary who sells to the highest bidder."

"What was he selling?" I asked.

"You."

I was white with fear; the blood drained from my face.

"What do they want with me?" I asked.

"I know all about you, Mateo. You are no financial wizard. You are a defector selling to the highest bidder. We know about you and the work you do. You are a nuclear physicist and you were heading the team working on fusion development. We know all about it. What you are doing could destroy world peace," Jasmin said, "The world would never be safe again if a rogue nation got hold of the tracker beam laser. We know it tracks nuclear submarines and ships by the radioactive waste and the new radar-inspired atomic ray would destroy them leaving no deterrent around the world. They are trying to kidnap you to get the information. Once they have it, Mateo, you will be of no use to them and you will be terminated. The British have kept this one to themselves. No other nation is involved in this. You are at risk of being kidnapped and sold to the highest bidder. Your plan did not work. You are the item they are bidding for; I am your only hope of getting out of here alive. I fell in love with you, Mateo. Now if I don't get you on the submarine in twenty-four hours, they will terminate me as well."

"How can this be, Jasmin? What are you?" I said screaming at her.

"I am a US Navy Seal, Mateo. I have come here on a mission to capture or kill you. I am going against my own government to protect you as they are actively trying to capture you themselves."

It turns out Jasmin was a commander in the US Navel special warfare Delta force. She was an active Navy Seal trained in armed multi-weapon combat, hand to hand field combat and an expert in global espionage. She was the head of her section; a lethal weapon. A true and active widow maker. Her code name: Malak the Destroyer. She had earned the name. She was the shadow on the wall, the sun ray on the fence, but you never saw her until it was too late. By then, you had been terminated. Jasmin had a one hundred percent kill record. A one of a kind silent but deadly assassin. She took no prisoners.

"Hurry. We have to get out of here fast. There will be others and I may not be able to protect you," she said. "I noticed the four men in the bakery. I recognised two of them. They are psychotic killers. They are a splinter group working as mercenaries. They work as a team. They will be on the payroll to get you back to the Eastern Bloc. Mateo, every nation is desperate to have the laser. You are just a pawn. It's time you woke up and smelt the coffee. Your life is hanging on a thread. Get with the programme and start thinking where we can go to get out of here."

"I have a sister in Tuscany. In the hills. Nobody will find us there. Maybe if we get the train to Nice, carry on to Rome, then transfer. We can be there by tomorrow night," I said.

"Okay, that's not a bad plan, but we will have to make sure we are not followed. They are going to be on us and we have to be a step ahead to ensure our safety and your sister's."

"I will phone her and let her know we are coming."

"No, Mateo, not from your phone. Make no more calls from that and get rid of your credit cards. We will be okay. I have money in a secret account I can access. Those following us are going to be ruthless and relentless. The money on your head is in the tens of millions. Every nuclear country is hell bent on getting the technology. It's a game of death they are playing. Those without it will have no nuclear deterrent as there will be no hiding from the tracker laser."

We made our way back to the hotel.

"Mateo, we need to talk," Jasmin said, "We have to have a plan to get us out of here. I've been thinking. We need to get train tickets at Antibes station. We might be able to get them online but we will have to pick them up at the station. You go in and get them whilst I have a look around. We have to be vigilant or you will end up in a communist country being tortured or at the best you will be dead. Your capture is paramount and they will not stop until they have you, Mateo. We will get the train at the next stop. It's too dangerous to catch it in Antibes. Too many agents are watching you. We are going to have to leave it until the last minute to get on in case we are being followed."

At the hotel, I went to reception to ask about check out notice. Jasmin said she would go up to the room. Jasmin chose to take the staircase in place of the lift. She was on a mission to make sure the approach to the room was safe.

She exited into the hallway; her hands were all cut and grazed.

"What happened?" I asked.

She said a man had approached her on the stairs and demanded she step down and leave Mateo to them. There was a scuffle. The man attacked her and she terminated him. Jasmin had rushed up the stairs as she thought there could be more and she wanted to know I was safe.

"I am okay, Jasmin. Come into the room and let's lock the door. We will leave early in the morning," I said.

Jasmin had been so gentle, loving and passionate yet she had turned into this ball of fire that seemed to consume everything in its way. I now had a volcanic killer. She was dangerous and explosive. I was glad she was on my side; I would not want her as an enemy. Jasmin was my protector. We were in trouble and I was out of my depth.

Jasmin sat there cleaning her gun ensuring reliability. She was fully focused on the job ahead. The love we had was stronger than ever. We were both fighting as a team. We were joined together and nobody was going to part us. I had decided I couldn't hide behind Jasmin. I had to be upfront and fight together. I had some combat experience as I had spent five years training in martial arts but never had to use it in a life-or-death situation.

Jasmin had been watching the news on the television. They had found the body of the mercenary in the harbour. They had it down as an accidental death, so the Sûreté

Nationale, also known as the French police, were not looking for us. But was someone covering for us? Who was it?

Jasmin pushed the chest of drawers to the door blocking it and said, "Let's get some sleep. We have a big day tomorrow."

Chapter 11

Mateo

Jasmin woke up and in a quiet voice said, "Come on, Mateo. It's 6am. We need to go before we become visible. We have to make that first train at 7am."

I asked the reception to call a taxi, "Tell them to meet us around the corner from the hotel, by the restaurant where they have the parrots in the cages."

Jasmin and I hurried out the hotel and made our way round the corner.

"Damn, the taxi is not here," I said.

"Come into the doorway so nobody can see us," Jasmin said, but just in time the taxi turned up.

We rushed into it and she said, "Drive to the railway station please."

"The railway station in Antibes?" he replied.

"No," said Jasmin, "The next one."

The driver drove off and it took around twenty minutes to get there but it was closed for repairs.

In a hurried voice, Jasmin said, "Driver, go to Nice station and drop us there. Can you make it quick? We have a connecting train to catch." Jasmin kept looking around to see if we were being followed. "I think we are okay. We have left them."

We arrived at Nice train station. It was an old colonial style station but it was all digital payments with machines and we had to queue to use them. I was sweating and we asked what train we needed for Milano.

The attendant said, "The Amalfi coast train to Sorrento."

That was a long way down the coast and we needed to change but were not sure when.

"Platform four, the 9.40am to Sorrento," the attendant said.

"Thank you," said Jasmin. "Let's stay obscure on the platform until they announce the train is on its way."

We looked at everybody that looked at us as mercenaries. Everyone was a possible threat to us. We sat there waiting for the train. It seemed ages and we were getting more fidgety as every minute went by.

"Mateo, sit down," Jasmin said as I got up to stretch my legs. "You will bring attention to us and that's the last thing we need at this moment."

I sat down as they announced the train to Sorrento via Milano.

"Good," I said.

"Let's go to the platform," she said.

We walked at a steady pace along the passenger tunnels passing the other platforms and we stood on the platform behind a couple and a child hiding from view of platform one. My heart was beating fast as we saw the train coming into the station.

"Mateo, let's get on at the rear of the train. I will get on first to make sure it is clear and you get on behind me as the train is pulling off."

As the train started to pull away, Jasmin saw two men running towards me. They lunged at me to stop me getting on the train.

"Run. Run, Mateo, hurry."

I was running for my life. Could I run fast enough to get on the train? I had to run faster. I found energy I never knew I had. Jasmin had her arm stretched out of the door. I pushed that bit further and grabbed her hand. She pulled me up onto the train. Looking back, the two men reached into their jackets for their guns but it was too late. We were both on the train.

"Wow, that was a close call," I said.

"Yes," said Jasmin, "You were nearly staying there in Nice."

We both let out a sigh of relief.

"Let's find our seats," I replied.

We sat down and Jasmin took my hand.

"Mateo, I love you so much it hurts."

I said, "I love you more. You are the best."

We settled down and about an hour later, the conductor came into the carriage. We asked him if the train went to Milano.

"No," he said, "You will have to change."

We needed to get as far away from Nice even if we had to backtrack. Jasmin looked and smiled at the conductor.

"Can we change our tickets please to Sorrento?"

The train conductor issued new tickets and said have a safe journey and continued through the carriage. As we looked at him moving towards the next carriage, I caught a glimpse of a man looking through the adjoining carriage window on the connecting door. It was one of the men from Antibes. He must have gotten on the train believing we were making a run for it.

I nudged Jasmin and said, "We have been followed."

Jasmin opened her bag on the floor and said, "We have fourteen and a half hours to go. We will sort it before the train pulls into Sorrento." Jasmin was looking to terminate them both; they always travelled together. Another scumbag would not be far away.

"Mateo, we have worked out a plan. You will have to distract one of them, make it look like we are splitting up. Me here and you in the rear carriage. We will have to guess where the other one is. I think they are working their way through the train, one from the front and one from the back. If you can find and distract one, it will give me a chance to terminate the other and then we can finalise the other mercenary between us."

She took her handbag and started going through the carriages to the front. I got up and made my way to the rear. I was fearful for Jasmin as we went our separate ways. I went into the last carriage and I could see nobody. Jasmin must have gotten it wrong; they were both at the front. I turned and ran through from carriage to carriage, passing the carriage where we sat. I raced through to the front to see an empty carriage with two men fighting Jasmin. She was like a wolf fighting a bear off of her pups, inflicting vicious bites to the animal.

The men were fighting back and Jasmin was weakening. Fighting two men in close confinement in hand-to-hand combat was too much as they were also trained like Jasmin. I ran up and pulled one off of Jasmin. I shoved my fingers in his eyes. He was screaming. I could see Jasmin. She was fighting hard to stay alive. She was the best. The man was twice her size but he was fighting a tiger. She was something else.

It was her and him now and it was to the detriment of the mercenary. I put my arm around the neck of the other mercenary from the rear. I had to end his life before he ended ours. I felt the air leaving his body as I tightened the grip. His body started to lose consciousness and his muscles relaxed. I had to make sure he had gone. I threw him to one side and pushed his own knife into his throat causing a gush of air and blood when I pulled the knife out. It was all over for him. He would be sleeping with the angels from now on.

I could see Jasmin was now outside between the coaches fighting. He was a big man. I went out to help her finish him. I could see he was hanging between the carriage coupling mechanism. Jasmin was trying to kick him off onto the track but he was hanging on. She let go of him, turned and kicked him in the face. Her high heel pierced his eye, and the stiletto broke off her shoe in his eye socket. She booted him again and he fell under the train screaming.

She shouted, "Every dog has its day and he has had his."

The other mercenary was dead on the floor of the carriage.

"Give me a hand," she said as she opened the window and threw the other one out onto the oncoming track. We made our way back to our seats.

"It was a good thing the train was not too busy," I said. I sat down and Jasmin put her arm around me.

"I feel tired and bruised," she said.

I held her and said she had done so well. She dropped into a deep sleep as we spoke. I held her and kissed her on the forehead.

"Me and you, darling, forever." She was the best thing I had ever known. "Sleep tight, my sweetheart. You have earned it."

Was I responsible for all this? The deaths, the chase, the danger? I looked at Jasmin. The bruising was starting to come out. I blamed myself. If I had only gotten to her quicker, she might not be in this way. After all, she had taken on two trained psychotic killers and won. What a woman I was holding. She was like a python and a leopard both fighting for their lives. One had to be the winner but at what cost?

We had to get off the train as soon as possible. Someone must have seen what happened. We could not be arrested as this would endanger us and everybody around us. We had to transfer to another train. I looked out the windows and saw a sign that said Tuscany was sixty kilometres away. I had not been back there for a long time but it was closer than I thought. I would leave her asleep until we reached Tuscany.

Shortly after the automatic information announced we were coming into Tuscany, I woke Jasmin.

"Come on, darling. We are getting off here."

Jasmin wiped her eyes and said, "I am with you, baby. Let's go."

We arrived in Tuscany. The area was absolutely stunning with the rolling hills, meandering country roads, lush fields with wheat and barley growing in the splendour of the Tuscany sunlight. Giant cypress trees, tall and elegant, blowing in the wind, almost in a gentle ballroom waltz, cast shadows over the landscape. The fields of grapevines ripening in the baking sun produced a wonderful taste in the air of a mature wine. The mist rolling over the hills told a story. Wildflowers edged the barley fields like a picture frame. This was one of God's best places. Everything about it made me want to stay and never leave.

"This is the most beautiful place in the world. I am exuberated with everything here. It's paradise in the making," said Jasmin.

"Yes," I replied, "But we must move on. I think I saw one of the men from Antibes. I believe he has followed us. I can see him in the distance."

Jasmin looked over and said, "It's one of the mercenaries. Let's move it. Quick. We need to get out of here. We need to get back on that train. It's too dangerous here and we need to keep your sister safe. We can come back here another time. I want to have good memories of this place not nightmares where I have killed a person. Strangely enough, Mateo, I hate terminating people but we are a target and we have to defend ourselves."

The train had to be stopped for thirty minutes and was about to start moving. The whistle had been blown and we needed to get on fast. Jasmin was looking for the mercenary.

"We will have to kill him before he kills us. I feel he will try to shoot us as he will get paid however it turns out," Jasmin said.

We boarded the train and it gathered speed. We were on the way to Sorrento. We sat in the carriage and we could see the Italian police were on the train. We didn't know why. Were they looking for us or just moving between cities? We kept a low profile so as not to draw attention to ourselves. We settled down and Jasmin cuddled up to me. I could see her drifting; her eyes were closing.

"Go to sleep," I said. "I will look after you, my love."

Chapter 12

Mateo

The train sped by. It seemed to be more of a family affair with people playing cards and families playing board games. As we looked over, they were playing House Builder. They were getting excited as they were building their own house. You could see them stage building their own house and trying to race to put their roof on first to win. The young boy won against the adults. They were in rapture about it, shouting and screaming. It was like going back to the sixties in England. Everybody was communicating and having fun.

Jasmin slept, slept and slept. She must have been so tired but the gentle rocking of the train kept her sleeping. I was starting to close my eyes, but I opened them fast as I was guarding my woman and not making a very good job of it. I had to stay awake for both of us. I sat there looking at Jasmin. Her eyelashes were so long. She never wore anything false and was natural in every way. Her skin was so smooth. I could see and feel small bumps under her fabulous hair. I think they were scars from past fights. It was a good job she had thick hair to hide them. I thought back to the people we had killed and whether they had families and wives. They would not be seeing them again. I was sad for them but in war the good prevail and our hearts were in the right place. But they were following us and wanted to harm us, so effectively it was self-defence.

The journey was going to be around eleven hours. As the train sped along, we looked out the window at the Amalfi coast. The waves were crashing upon the rocks, the sea looked slightly rough. I was okay, I had my love at the side of me. What a change it had all been. It seemed rushed but it had all calmed down. I was relaxed and enjoyed the ride. I knew we still had things to sort out with the mercenary but that was on the back burner for now. All I wanted to do was enjoy the moment with my woman.

As the train stopped at stations, I looked out the window to see who was getting on. Would there be more mercenaries looking for a quick dollar to trade me and my secrets to a foreign power? We were in desperate times and it called for desperate measures. I looked out, but it seemed only families were leaving and boarding the train. Possibly holidaymakers setting off for Sorrento to enjoy the last of the autumn sun.

The whistle went and the train was off again. *Not too long now and we will be there*, I thought. Jasmin was stirring and waking up.

"Hello, baby. How are you?" she said in a sweet gentle voice.

"I am good, sweetheart. Did you have a good sleep?"

"Wonderful," she replied, "I really needed that. I was tired. I feel a bit bruised and battered. The fight was hard. He was a strong man."

"That's all behind you now."

"Yes, let's move on," she said and Jasmin leant over and kissed me on the lips, "Thank you."

"That was really nice of you."

"How far is it to Sorrento?" she asked.

"Not long," I replied. "We should be there in less than two hours. Let's go to the buffet carriage and have a drink. I think we are more than ready."

"Yes, that would be a good idea. I would like a toasted sandwich if they have one." Jasmin held my hand and continued onto the buffet carriage.

We chattered about the things we wanted to do in Sorrento.

"I always wanted to come to Italy but never seemed to have the time, but I am here now and really happy to be here with you, Mateo. And for us to be alive. We need to enjoy the time we have together," Jasmin said.

"Yes, we must. I have heard it's really nice here," I replied.

The announcement came across the speaker.

"We are approaching Sorrento station. Please make sure you have all your belongings before leaving the train."

We got up and made our way to the door. The station was small but efficient. We got off the train and made our way out, following the exit signs. It looked quaint with lots of old buildings and narrow streets. It was still warm and we agreed to look for a hotel first before dinner. We needed to get settled down somewhere and we would look for a nice restaurant later.

We managed to find a bijou hotel. It looked inviting with its stone exterior and all the lights were like a beacon showing us the way. We took a room on the first floor. It had beautiful high ceilings with a large cornice running around the ceiling with gold leaf edging the walls. It was very good for a place so small. Jasmin said she would like us to have a house like this in Italy. I think she had found her dream home. All she needed to do now was get married and fill it with children.

"Let's go out for dinner, my love. I need to satisfy my hunger for food and then my love." She moved over to me and grabbed me in a place only a man has and she said she was hungry for me, all of me.

I smiled and said, "You are my love. I am so happy you picked me. I want you. I want you to remember this night forever."

As we walked to find a restaurant, it was getting dark. Jasmin was really horny and kept on touching me in an inappropriate place and wanting to be kissed on every corner of every street and there were lots. Our lips were dry by the time we found a restaurant.

I walked in with Jasmin; she was holding on my arm like it was going somewhere without her. I smiled at the waiter.

"Have you a table for two please? And some ice water to cool my darling down please," I said.

Jasmin was hot and she showed it.

The waiter said, "What a lucky man you are. Can I have just a bit of your luck?"

Jasmin's emotions were running wild, as she whispered, "Shall we leave the food and go back to the hotel? I want you so bad."

"It looks like there will be no sleep tonight," I replied. We ordered two large steaks. Jasmin never took her eyes off of me all night. It felt so good to have a woman so devoted to me.

We had eaten and started making our way back to the hotel. We got to the room door and Jasmin held me against it. Her hands were going everywhere. We were kissing and I was excited as I put my hands around all her beautiful assets, stroking her all over, caressing her whole body. She was excited crawling backwards on the door. I needed to get her inside the room so I could strip her off to see my woman. She was a piece of art, precious, sensual, sexy and loving me more than I could possibly deserve.

Getting into bed, she was taking control. She wanted to make love to me. This lady was an expert in almost everything. She knew how to push the buttons. Every moment was one of ecstasy. We were sliding around it was that good. The whole world was ours for the taking. I think if God was looking over us, he would have shut one eye but Jasmin might have opened them both.

I don't think there was an inch of Jasmin's body I had not visited in the moment. I could taste her on my lips. It was like she had an insatiable appetite for love and the more she got, the more she wanted. She worked on me most of the night ensuring satisfaction every time. Jasmin seemed to have a different fetish for everywhere we made love. She loved having her long hair pulled. She said it turned her on.

"I like pulling your hair as well," I replied.

Jasmin laughed, "So, you are as bad as me."

"Only with you, my love."

We made love in so many positions. I did not think the human body could bend like that, but Jasmin said it satisfied the fire burning within her. Now she was scorching hot. I was experiencing the best love ever; she was breaking all the records. There was no holding back with her. She was an explorer and nothing was impossible.

She was out to discover true love and all the beauty it encompassed.

Jasmin was love without limits. The love she showed for me was indescribable. I could not put it into words. It seemed her energy was endless and relentless. She was as beautiful on the inside as the outside. Where had this woman been all my life? Were we really meant to be?

Chapter 13

Mateo

The next morning, we slept well. Jasmin had slept wrapped around me. As I woke up, I could tell she was dreaming as I could see her closed eyes rolling, like searching for a place for adventure.

I gazed at her thinking how my woman was full of so much mystery. What was she dreaming about? Was it love or something more sinister? She tightened her grip on me. She wrestled with herself. This was not a love scene but more of a thriller. I comforted her and she seemed to settle a bit. As I moved to get out of bed, she woke.

"Good morning, baby. I love you," she said.

"Good morning, my love. I love you more. Did you have a nice dream?"

"I was in a dark place and could not find my way out. I was panicking and then I woke up. It felt so good when I saw you there."

We continued down to breakfast and discussed where we were going for the day.

Jasmin said, "I would like to go to the beach."

"There's no beach here, baby," I laughed, "It's all rock face but they do have bathing platforms. They are really nice."

"I would love to go and sit on one of them. I love to see the water."

We made our way down the staircase to the platform; it was busy with a small cove with people swimming in it. Jasmin took her clothes off and lay on the bathing platform in her bikini. It seemed everybody was looking at her as she was definitely a head-turner. She liked and enjoyed the attention. Jasmin asked if I would apply the suntan cream.

"Will you make sure you rub it in well?" she added.

Well, there was a clear message. I enjoyed the moment as I massaged it into her beautiful skin.

"Mateo, your hands are so strong," she said.

I laughed and said, "That was only the start."

The autumn sun was nice. Not too hot but really soothing.

Jasmin said, "I would love to go for a swim in that water."

At the same moment, she got up and dived in the water. My heart sank as I saw her swim away.

"Come on," she shouted, "Come in, Mateo."

I watched her as she swam. She was a professional swimmer; her style was like an Olympic swimmer. How could she now swim like this, yet in the river she was drowning? I let myself into the water and began to swim with her. She was a strong swimmer. I thought we needed to talk when we exited the water.

Jasmin said the water was getting cold but she had been about fifty yards out from the shore, swimming like a fish. My thoughts were racing. Who was this woman? She seemed good at everything she did. Was she a natural or had she been trained? How could she swim now but was drowning before? I struggled to get my head around it as Jasmin climbed back out to the bathing platform.

"Mateo, can you dry me with the towel?" she asked.

As I dried her, my mind was on overtime. How could this woman be so different and hard to understand?

We walked back up to the hotel to get changed, ready for a day of sightseeing. Jasmin wanted to visit Capri so I booked the boat and we walked down to the jetty. Jasmin was excited. She had never been there but always wanted to see all of Italy. I was still thinking and concerned where all this was taking us. I needed to speak about it but did not want to ruin the day.

We got off the boat in Capri and I said, "All the shops are at the top of the island."

"It looks a long way up," she replied.

"It will be a nice walk."

As we walked, we took in all the views. The streets were really steep with little cottage-style houses dotted along the way. It was very tranquil. Jasmin was asking questions all the way up to the top, where we rounded the top of the island.

Jasmin's eyes opened wide and she shouted, "Look at all these beautiful shops. It's every girl's dream. Designer shops... who would have believed it? They have all the top designers here. Can I have a look, my love?"

"Of course," I replied, "How could you miss out on this."

Jasmin was trying everything on in the shops. I watched her. She was like a child in a sweet shop and she wanted to taste everything. She was not coming out without a new wardrobe of clothes. We carried out three bags. We were loaded down but I knew it made her happy and her being happy made me smile. She was so lovely. We were enjoying the time together.

As we made our way down the hill, there were crowds of people lining the roads. Jasmin asked what was happening.

"It's an annual race to the bottom of the island," I told her.

"Let's watch it, Mateo. I want to see it."

"It's a bit scary. They come down on wooden sledges and have to use their wooden clogs to turn the corners and try to stop. It's very fast and steep."

Putting her arm around my neck, she said, "I love it. If it's dangerous, I like it. I love you so much, Mateo. Every day, I wake up loving you. And when I go to sleep, you are the last thought in my head. You are my life now, Mateo."

Jasmin held me around my waist. There were crowds of people. Jasmin was all over me. I wanted her. She seemed relentless. She was having me and I had no choice. We did about everything but remove our clothes. She was burning up and I was the fuel firing her. Looking at her, I was melting. She was the fabulous woman I met on a train. I was ready for passion and love with her. Whatever she was, I would accept her. After all, love conquers all.

We walked to the jetty and cruised back to Sorrento. The water was calm and it made the trip pleasant.

Jasmin kissed me and said, "Thank you, darling. I have had a wonderful day."

It was around 6pm and the sun was disappearing over the horizon. As we walked up from the jetty, we could see Sorrento lit up in all its glory. It looked like somewhere off of a postcard. It was enchanting. We had decided to eat in the hotel as there was a tapas night. Jasmin said it was something she had never tried but would like to. She was inquisitive as to what we might be eating.

"Don't worry, it's lots of different dishes. There will be lots there you will like," I said. I linked arms and kissed her as we walked back to the hotel.

"Who lives behind these large gates? Why are they so high?"

"There are often gardens or courtyards behind them and they are for privacy. There are sometimes very well-kept gardens with citrus trees and exotic plants," I explained.

Jasmin asked me how I knew. I told her that I'd had a girlfriend in Rome that lived in a similar place. Jasmin was not happy and seemed jealous.

I laughed and said, "I was only nineteen years old at the time."

She smiled and we resumed the conversation.

We arrived back at the hotel and Jasmin held me in the revolving door.

"We are not getting out till you tell me you love me and want to marry me and have your children," she said. She was not going to let the door go.

"You don't need to lock me in, Jasmin. I love you now and I will love you forever."

A tear appeared in her eyes as she said, "I will love you forever as well."

I put my arms round her and hugged her.

"Mateo, you are the best man I have ever had the pleasure to meet. Never mind, love. You are my saviour and I love you for that."

There was a queue at the door and we moved into the foyer, booked our table and went to our room to get ready for the night. I wanted to have a talk with Jasmin but now was not the right time. Would there ever be a right time? I had to talk to her and soon, but tonight belonged to Jasmin.

The waiter asked if we wanted to sit outside in the courtyard overlooking the sea.

"I have a lovely table for a beautiful lady," the waiter added.

Jasmin smiled and said, "Yes, please."

She looked beautiful in her designer dress. It was a tight-fitting ballroom style black lace and diamond dress. She made the dress look good. It looked so good it could have been made to fit her. She looked like she was in Hollywood ready to accept an Oscar. It showed every perfect curve of her body. She was wearing the bracelet she bought in St Tropez.

As she looked at it, she said, "Darling, I loved St Tropez. It was beautiful."

"Not as beautiful as you, my love."

We ordered a bottle of red wine: Cabernet Sauvignon. Jasmin asked to be excused from the table to use the toilet. As she got up from the seat, my eyes were cast over her calves; the shape of her legs was slender. The stockings were black with a darker line down the back of them, down to her high heels which were black and rear open. I struggled to see how she could keep them on but she walked perfectly. All eyes were on Jasmin. She knew how to stop a crowd and she made sure she did. She made me slightly nervous. She was mine and I did not want someone taking her away from me. It was like holding a large diamond, looking at its beauty then having to give it back. I felt Jasmin was only on loan and I would have to give her away one day.

"Hello, baby. You are back," I said as Jasmin sat down.

"I am hungry," she said.

"I will order the tapas then."

"It's you I am hungry for, Mateo. I want your body," she whispered as she rubbed legs with me under the table.

I remembered getting a glimpse of her coming out of the bathroom earlier; her long legs and lace underwear. She looked amazing. Her 34C breasts, like perfect hills nestled into her charcoal bra. Her thong seemed to part the cheeks in exactly the right place and make her look like she was going out without them on. Was I dreaming? Jasmin spoke as I recovered from my gaze into the past hour. My mind was wandering. We both knew exactly what she was wearing underneath that stunning dress. I nearly lost the conversation.

"Are you all right, Mateo?" Jasmin asked.

"Oh yes. I am okay. Just thinking about something."

"Anything I can help you with?" Jasmin replied.

"No, thank you, darling. Just thinking about family."

"Okay, my love. Have you ordered?"

"Yes, we are having a selection of tapas the waiter suggested."

"I am looking forward to it," she said smiling.

I poured the wine and we toasted to good luck and happiness and love always. We looked each other in the eyes and drank some wine. For a split second, I was mesmerized looking into her eyes. They seemed to change colour depending on the light. It looked as if I was looking at a firework exploding in the sky. Her eyes were encaptivating. The tail ends of the firework reflected them in the dark sky. Her pupils were not visible. They had been taken over by the sparkle of the comet as it fizzled out. Until the next burst came into her eyes. Was Jasmin really mine? I felt insecure. My emotions were not in a good place at the moment. I was sure of nothing apart from my love for Jasmin.

The waiter turned up with the food.

"What a feast!" Jasmin said as he laid it on the table. We managed to eat half of it. The food was excellent. We finished the wine and we walked outside the hotel. We agreed to go for a walk along the cliff road to let the food settle. We joked and laughed although I wanted to ask some questions. We were too happy to spoil the moment. We gazed at the stars shining over the waves crashing against the rocks below. It was a beautiful moment. We were so close. We were more in love than ever.

We meandered our way back to the hotel. We held each other in a caring way and dropped to sleep. It seemed the lust Jasmin had earlier turned to love and took her over.

Chapter 14

Mateo

The night went fast. It was soon morning. I got up and opened the blinds. The sun was shining over the Mediterranean Sea. There was a boat race taking place. The yachts had their colours on the masts showing in all their glory. You could see them racing around the island. They looked so good. I saw Jasmin was getting out of bed. She looked more interesting than the yachts. They did not have her figure, curves or sexy looks. Her hair almost touched the top of her bottom. She came over.

"Good morning, honey. Have I told you I love you?" she said.

"I love you more," I replied.

As she held me in a passionate embrace, she said, "Look, Mateo. Look at the yachts. Are they racing?"

"Yes," I replied.

"I would like to be on one of them racing around the island. I used to sail, Mateo."

"Jasmin, you seemed to have so much in your life. We need to sit and find out about each other."

"I am up for that, my darling," Jasmin said. "For you, it's time we come clean with each other."

"Okay, Jasmin, let's talk. Who are you?"

"Does it really matter who I am, Mateo?"

"Yes. To me it does, Jasmin."

"I told you earlier… I am a US Navy Seal. I am here to protect you from an enemy too scary to tell you. And where you might end up? Possibly in an eastern country and at the worst a communist one. I never boarded that train in London. The train had left five minutes after I arrived there. British secret service air lifted me by helicopter to Calais train station. You were asleep. We removed the man in the seat across the aisle so I could be near you when you woke up. My mission was to take you on board a US submarine or, failing that, terminate you. The British are aware you are defecting from the UK and selling information to the highest bidder. This was never going to happen as the stakes are too high. I just happened to fall in love with you and my love is no lie. I truly love you, Mateo, but I need to make sure you are safe. You have no idea what you have done. These are ruthless governments that stop at nothing to get what they want.

It's imperative they catch and contain you; they will stop at nothing until they achieve their goal."

She took a deep breath and continued.

"Are you so blind not to see this coming? Did you actually think you would come out of this with your life? When they have you, they will enslave you until they have all the information and all the formulas and the know-how they need. They will terminate you to stop anybody else obtaining the weapon. Its paramount they don't get the weapon through you. I cannot let them take you alive. I have been looking after your wellbeing since Leon. Yes, I can swim, Mateo. I am an excellent swimmer. After all, I am a Navy Seal. The river boat was a diversion, my love. I had to sort out some business with two Asian killers. I could not do what I did whilst you were there. They died a gruesome death but it had to be done. They were making moves to terminate me and sell you. You were not aware; I needed the time alone to do my job."

She took my hand into hers as she spoke.

"The hospital was a diversion like the drowning in the river. I am sorry I deceived you but I had to ensure our safety. I also had to order certain equipment I needed for our survival. There are a lot of agents after you. There is a price on your head and it's gone global. You are a bounty to everybody looking to cash you in. This could be more dangerous than the 1962 Cuban missile crisis. The world will be on its highest alert if this is lost to a rogue nation. I need to move you somewhere safer; I have noticed agents from five different countries whilst we have been here. They are keeping a low profile and biding their time till they can strike."

"Jasmin, I can help."

"Mateo, you have been out of your depth ever since you boarded the train in London. You need to always stay close to me. Do not move out of my sight. Your life depends on it. Death is final, Mateo. Please remember that. We have to get out of here fast, Mateo. I need you to stay here and get ready to come out to me when I call you."

Jasmin left the hotel with a new black rucksack on her back as I waited for her call.

Suddenly, there was a massive explosion at the harbour. One boat literally lifted into the sky in a ball of flames. At that, a car screeched round the corner.

Jasmin shouted, "Get in, Mateo. Get in the car. Hurry."

She took off like a F14 fighter jet, screeching around the narrow streets. Heading up the coastline back towards Tuscany. I felt like we were flying. Where did she learn to drive like that? We managed to leave the costal road onto a motorway. I was glad. We were going so fast that I was feeling the sensation you get on the biggest rollercoaster you have ever been on. My stomach did not know whether it was coming or going, I was feeling that sick. I was definitely on that ride. I spent the next ten minutes with my head out the window. It was a sick moment for Jasmin as she kept on taking the electric window up and down with my head in it. She said it was funny and it broke the silence in the car.

"Did you see that explosion in the harbour, Jasmin?" I asked.

"Yes," she replied, "I had to create a diversion and so I put a bomb on the boat. It worked. I don't think anybody saw us drive out of there."

"Wow. So, you were responsible for that boat, Jasmin?"

"Yes, Mateo. A small price to pay for our short-term freedom." Jasmin pulled over to the side of the road. "You drive, Mateo. I need to consult on who might have seen us and who could be on their way to intercept us. We need to put some kilometres between us to give us time to think and put a plan in place. I think now would be the right time to hide out at your sister's. It's not safe on the train or in the cities. We will take it in turns to drive whilst one of us sleeps. We will be there tomorrow."

"Where did you get the car?" I asked.

"Don't ask, Mateo. You don't want to know."

I looked forwards and shook my head in disbelief.

"So, we have someone's car?"

"Yes, Mateo. It's ours now. We could say it was on loan to us." Jasmin smiled and leant over and kissed me. "Don't worry, baby. They will get it back later."

"Do we need fuel, Jasmin?"

"No, Mateo. I stole one that was full," she laughed. "Well, we will leave a tip."

I smiled. At least we were safe, and on the road to see my sister.

"You will like her and she will love you, Jasmin," I said.

The car was very small; not something Jasmin was used to. Living in America, everything was big over there. She cuddled up beside me and was playing with me. She was horny and wanted me to pull over somewhere. Cars were flashing by as there was nowhere to pull over. Jasmin floated the idea that she would be able to relieve me. I knew what that meant.

I said, "That's the last thing we need. The police pulling us over for indecent exposure."

Jasmin was laughing uncontrollably. She found it really funny.

"You are a darling, Mateo. You are always thinking about the consequences in place of the fun. I love you so much. My anchor, stabilising me."

"Well, someone has to keep my woman under control."

"Yes, master," she replied laughing.

We saw a sign for fuel and rest facilities.

"We need fuel and something to eat," I said.

"You fill up, Mateo, whilst I get two coffees and some pastries for our lunch."

As I looked over to the bakery, I could not see Jasmin. I began to panic, where was she? Jasmin had disappeared. I paid for the fuel and parked the car in a space in front of the bakery.

I looked over to the hedge behind the garage to see Jasmin smashing a rock into a man's head; there had been a bloody battle. Jasmin was covered in blood. I ran over and grabbed her by the arm.

"Are you okay, baby?" I asked.

"Yes," she said, "But that turd is not breathing any more air."

The grass was unkept and partially hid the body. It was the last of the four mercenaries from the south of France. She had totalled them all. The fear was how many were out there looking for us that we did not know about and were they a step up from the last four. I kept a look out whilst Jasmin went to the restroom to clean up. I gave her some clean clothes to wear. She said she would have to take her old ones with us as it would incriminate us if anyone found them around the crime scene. She said we would dispose of them later. She was upset as the blouse she had been wearing was a new one she bought in Capri and now it was ruined.

We walked to the car and made our way back onto the motorway. It had been a bad experience. As we drank our coffee, it helped us relax for the onward journey.

Chapter 15

Jasmin

I reached out holding onto Mateo's hand and softly said, "I truly love you, Mateo. With all my heart. Nothing is more important in my life than our happiness. I want to live all my life with you."

I looked into his eyes and enquired about where his parents met.

"They met in Tuscany after national service. He was a captain in the horse guards and my mother met him on a public parade. He was a true gentleman; so handsome and charming. He seemed to have a silver tongue. Every word he spoke seemed to catch my mother's attention. She was so happy. It was like she had died and was reborn again. It was a magic moment in her life, she told me. He doted on her and loved her more than the day before. He made sure she had fresh flowers every day as he knew she loved flowers. He said she was his beautiful moment and he wanted to make her have the best day today and every day. They had never had any bad feelings between them and their love for each other was their gift to me from them both."

Tears formed in my eyes as he continued to story.

"I have always tried to live up to the warmth and love they gave to me. I felt so honoured to be their child and still do. And although they are not here now, they are in my heart every day, from when I wake up until I go to sleep. My mother said love was endless. I was not sure what she was trying to tell me, but I realise that she was right as it is never ending and I would like to share the love they shared with someone I love. My parents spent a lot of time in Tuscany and had a favourite restaurant. It was quaint, not too posh, but the place had a presence of joy about it and my mother picked up on this as it was their place. It was high on a hill and overlooked fields of barley. My mother said it was sun-kissed by the lord himself. She said it was a heavenly place and by being there she felt closer to God. It was the place my father proposed to my mother. It was the happiest day of her life; they did not seem to want much out of life but each other. They had found each other, and they were never letting go. Only death could part them, but they knew they would be together again one day."

"They were really in love. I want my life to be the same as theirs. Your parents were so lucky to have found the love they had."

I told Mateo the story was beautiful but heart-wrenching, and asked if I could go back to the room for a lie down as I wanted to be somewhere calm with him.

"Mateo, I want exactly what they had." Mateo's name was a gift from the gods. I had not told Mateo on the train to Paris as I was not sure if he would believe me. He was so proud of the meaning of his name, but my name meant exactly the same. Jasmin was also a gift from the gods. What was the chance that our names would have the same meaning? We were meant for each other.

This was not just coincidence; God had bought us together. As I thanked God under my breath, I decided I was not going to tell Mateo until the time was right.

Mateo was a nuclear physicist working as a scientist in the UK on fusion development. He had been heading a team developing a fusion laser capable of taking out any ships or submarines within a three hundred mile radius using a tracker beam laser. A new radar-inspired atomic ray that could track nuclear radiation omitted from the nuclear-powered ships and submarines and destroy them. They were going into production of a prototype when Mateo Grimshaw disappeared. He had been under surveillance for a long time by MI5 due to co-ordinates of the tracker beam laser being retracked to the Pacific Ocean off the west coast of the USA. We believed he was working with a rogue nation but had no concrete evidence to isolate him from the development and production of the tracker beam laser. There had been activity on Mateo Grimshaw registering bank accounts in the Cayman Islands under a company name and the directors did not exist and were ghost directors. He had bought a Eurostar open ticket for France and Europe. He had telephoned in sick for seven days and had made his way to St Pancras International train station. He stopped at a coffee bar for a panini and a coffee, and he continued his journey to Paris. MI5 was evident in conjunction with the CIA with me as commander: Jasmin Watson.

I boarded the train at Calais en route to Paris. Our object was to find out who the rogue nation was, who was funding Mateo Grimshaw and why he had turned rogue. This technology was supreme in warfare as it could destroy ships and submarines and it was going to be installed in British satellites. The implications of the technology getting into the wrong hands would be a catastrophe and would end the deterrent of nuclear-powered warships and submarines patrolling the earth as a peace keeping force. We had to find any papers and destroy the rogue nation's capability of obtaining this weapon. We had to find the contacts of Mateo Grimshaw and who he was working for. We were looking for the head of the snake; we had to cut it off for the sake of world peace. We were both in deep water. We had to learn how to swim and fast.

"It would have been nice to take you to Rome," Mateo said, "It's a fabulous city and the Vatican is something else. If we get through all this, Jasmin, I will take you to Rome."

"I would love that, Mateo," I replied. "How long to Tuscany?"

"It's around three hours to where my sister lives. Should we call her?"

"No, just in case our phones are being monitored. The people chasing us are powerful and could have access to our phone conversations. We cannot afford to give away our location."

A rogue government had sent in four agents to track and monitor Mateo. Foreign powers needed the technology out of his head. All the major countries in the world wanted this radar-inspired atomic ray and were going to be ruthless and relentless to possess it. It seemed every nuclear country in the world was hell bent on stealing the technology. They were not working with me so I made sure they were all terminated. Only I would be getting a pay day. Mateo was not in the running for anything. Mateo was just a pawn in a game and just a commodity dispensable at a moment's notice. But all this had now changed. Now love was the only thing on my mind.

We were near as we saw a sign saying, "Tuscany". All we had to do was find Mateo's sister's house. He said it was on top of a hill overlooking a valley. It was not far away now. The area we were in took my breath away. It was so beautiful. Only the lucky people lived here. It had a peaceful look about it. The small stone-built houses took you back to ancient times in your mind and made you expect a horse and cart to appear in front of you with a load of hay. It was as if time had stood still.

Mateo looked up, pointed into the distance and said, "There it is, the family home."

"Wow, it's a long way off. It looks lonely up there."

"Yes, Jasmin. That's the way my mother and father wanted it. They loved the solitude of it and the beauty that surrounded it. There is a big valley facing south and there are some lavender fields below. The smell in the evening is magnificent. It makes you want to stay out all night especially on a breezy warm night. The cypress trees seem to put on a show dancing in formation. You can see the hawks soaring, catching the thermals over the top of the valley, looking for an evening meal. No need for TV there, Jasmin. Just use your senses and take everything in."

As we went through the village, I was excited. It was a beautiful village.

"I want to live here please, Mateo."

"Yes, my darling, I am sure we will live here one day."

"One day, Mateo? I need this now. I love it here. I can see myself sitting out here with the sun caressing me on my body." I wanted to stop. "Mateo, can we stay here and have a glass of wine? Please, darling."

"Of course," he replied.

We parked and walked to a small bar with seating outside. I wanted to sit out in the sun to realise my dream of being able to live here. We found a table that overlooked the valley at the rear of the bar.

"What a stunning view," I said, "It's just like you portrayed it, beautiful. I could live and die here; I don't want any more than this. I am so happy, Mateo. Just me and you here sounds like heaven."

"Same for me as well," Mateo replied. "We need to make our way to the house as we need to settle in before it's late and my sister is not expecting us as we could not phone. She will be worried who is coming up the drive."

Chapter 16

Mateo

As we drove up the drive, it was flanked by cypress trees lining the sides. Jasmin was taken back and she was stuttering to get the words out.

"It's amazing. It's like something out of a film. It's so amazing, it doesn't seem real. I've never been anywhere like this."

"My father planted the trees the year they inherited the house nearly fifty years ago and here we are with fully grown trees. Life comes and goes so fast. Sometimes you can't keep up with it. My sister lived here with her now-deceased husband, whilst I was in the US with my parents. They used to bring me here during holiday periods and they said they would retire here, and they did till the end."

As we got closer to the house, Jasmin had tearful eyes.

"It's so beautiful, Mateo. How could you not live here? I am crying with joy."

I saw my sister, Isabella, walking towards the car.

"Who is it?" she asked.

"Your brother, Mateo," I shouted.

"Mateo!" she cried running towards the car.

"My beautiful Isabella," I shouted. I stopped the car and we ran to each other into a colliding embrace. We had not seen each other since my parents died two years prior, but our blood was hot and thick and we were together again. We walked back towards the car.

"This is Isabella," I said introducing her to Jasmin.

"Nice to meet you. I'm Jasmin."

"Come on in, Jasmin," Isabella said, "We have lots to talk about."

We all walked towards the house. As Isabella opened the door, the house felt alive. It had a welcome feeling about it; this was home. Isabella had a lovely golden retriever who ran out wagging her tail.

"Her name is Bella," she said.

"Bella, come here," Jasmin called. Bella and Jasmin were an instant success. They both liked each other.

"You must both be hungry," Isabella said.

"Yes, we are. We have had a long drive. What are you thinking, Isabella?" I said.

"I have some cheeses, olives and fresh bread and, of course, wine from the vineyard."

"That would be lovely," I replied.

"You sit down with a glass of wine and I will see to the food."

We sat on the veranda overlooking the valley. The view was stunning. Just then, two fighter planes tore through the valley. The sound was deafening.

Jasmin said, "Quick. Hide, Mateo."

"Hell's teeth, I've never seen fighter planes here before," I said.

"I think they are reconnaissance planes; they are looking for us, Mateo. Keep out of sight or they will find us. We will have to keep indoors between noon and 2pm as the satellite will be dead above us at that time and they will be trying to focus in on us. They know we are here. It's just *where* they want to know. I am scared for us, my love."

In a moment, things had changed from tranquillity to unrest. It seemed the Italian air force was also involved for some reason. We had to lie low for a while. Hopefully they would move on somewhere else in their search. Could they have tracked the car from the service station? Had they found the body of the mercenary? Were they now tracking us through motorway cameras? They probably knew we had come off the motorway and were in this area.

"I don't think we can stay long here, Mateo. They are going to pull out all the stops to capture us. I'm afraid they are going to find us," Jasmin said. "I'm not sure how you are going to tell Isabella but we have to leave early morning before they find us here."

"I would like to tell her the truth but that would make her worry and I don't want her to. You will have to say you have had a call from your mother, Jasmin, and your father is ill. You need to get straight back as they think he is terminally ill. We will be on our way early morning. Let's dump the car on the other side of the valley and get on a bus to Milano. We might be able to lose ourselves in the city. Whilst there, we can think out a strategic plan as to where we can go, where we will be safe."

"Mateo, I don't think there is a place in the whole world where we will be safe. We will have to turn you in, but who dare we trust with our lives?"

I spoke to my sister. She said she was sad we were going so soon but understood that if Jasmin's father was poorly, we should go. I hated telling my sister a lie but needs must and we needed to get away from the area for her safety and ours. We kissed goodbye and we were on our way to the village.

We saw a car park so we parked the car in an obscure corner so as not to bring too much attention to it and we walked up to a bus stop to catch a bus. We were going to have to get an interconnecting bus to Milano. The local bus arrived and we were both glad to see it as we were exposed standing there for everyone to see. We needed to be away from prying eyes.

The bus meandered down the country roads. It was beautiful with the mist hanging over the fields like a fluffy blanket and the sun just trying to break through in the morning dawn. We were leaving one of God's best places.

Jasmin was looking everywhere; she was on guard. Every time the bus stopped, she looked up to see who was getting on. The way she was, I would not have liked to be the wrong person on this bus as she had fire in her eyes. It never left my thoughts she was a killer and the best in her class.

We got into the main bus station and we changed bus onto the Milano flyer. We should be okay now; not many stops on this one. Jasmin might be able to relax on the journey. The bus joined the motorway and we sat back. I could feel Jasmin's body relax into my arms. She was at peace for now. She looked so lovely asleep. It was the first time I had paid any attention to her sleeping. She was so at rest. A lot had happened in the last few days, it was exhausting. I loved this woman so bad it hurt. I wanted to protect her from the mercenaries but I was no match for my woman. She fought like a lion but was as soft as a rabbit tail.

I was honoured to have her love. We were going to get through all this. I was thinking if I could get back to the UK and give myself in to the authorities and keep the love of my life safe in England. I had made so many mistakes. How had I put myself in this position? I had dragged Jasmin into a dangerous game of cat and mouse. I couldn't keep relying on Jasmin to sort everything out. I had to man up and try to do something constructive but I was at a loss. I didn't even know my enemy or even what they looked like. It was not what I did. I was a nuclear physicist who had gone rogue. My greed had put me in a position I never knew about. My life was in danger and I couldn't see the light at the end of the tunnel, to exit the trouble we were in.

I could see the bus was coming towards the city. There was a lot of graffiti on the walls and all the trains were parked up. Were the Italians a race of graffiti artists? It looked like some futuristic film surviving after a nuclear war. My mind was somewhere else. Was I in that film as it seemed everything was being destroyed. I felt like we were alone fighting in a futuristic land under martial law fighting for survival, but we were in Italy. A civilised country. Yet we were being persecuted by foreign powers hell bent on kidnapping me. I was angry that they would dare try to take me away from here and from who I love.

I looked down at Jasmin. I felt tears appear in my eyes. What had I done to put us in so much danger? Why were people so ruthless?. It was all about money and power. What a terrible combination and I was instrumental in fuelling this myself. Who was I to judge anybody when I was as guilty of greed as the next man? I had chosen my own destiny without thinking first. I must have been mindless to do what I did. The end to this would be winner takes it all. I only hoped it was us and we would still have our lives. I felt so out of my depth. I was punching well above my weight. I was starting to show fatigue and I was wavering.

How long would we have to keep hiding? Were they ever going to call it a day and leave us alone? Jasmin started to stir; she was waking up. I thought only of another nightmare day for her. I was now of the opinion of shit or bust. I had tortured myself enough. I was getting ready to accept what was coming and I would defend my lady with my life if I had to. But we were fighting an enemy that was prepared for war. They were a step ahead of us. I only had my skills in martial arts to protect us. Totally no good against guns. They were fully tooled up for combat.

I looked at Jasmin and said, "Hello, tiger. You look absolutely beautiful, my love."

She smiled. That smile told a thousand words. We were in the best love film ever made. She was my leading lady and I wanted her to take centre stage so I could show this beautiful woman to the world. I kissed her passionately.

"Every man's dream. I have found love in a hopeless place."

Chapter 17

Mateo

As we came into the bus station, Jasmin went quiet.

"I think I've just seen somebody I know sitting down in the café as we went by," she said, "He was in the window. I am sure it was him. I remember him. He was a marine in the navy. I met him in New York about eighteen months ago on a mission. I wonder what he is doing here in Milano. He is a long way from home. He said New York was his last trip as he was retiring from the marines. It's strange to see him, he just looked out of place. I would have liked to hook up with him and see what he is doing in his retirement. I'm not definitely sure it was him but I will see if I can catch him when the bus stops."

We were just waiting for the bus to find a space to park. We exited the bus.

"Can we just go and see if it was the marine?" she asked.

"Yes, of course," I replied.

We hurried across the bus station to the café. If the marine had been sitting in that seat, he had gone now.

"How could he have gone so fast?" Jasmin said. "I was really looking forward to a catch up."

"Never mind," I said, "I'm sure you may see him again."

Milano was a big city. Probably little chance of ever meeting him again.

I said, "We may as well have a drink whilst we are here." I ordered two americanos and sat down. It was busy in the café. That was a good thing as we needed to blend in more. We could not afford to be transparent. We had to find somewhere to stay whilst we were here in Milano. I needed to be sure that our plan would not be compromised by anybody looking to trade us in.

We got into a taxi. We were going to a hotel near the Milano Cathedral which Jasmin had booked online. The hotel was accessed behind a large black wooden door. It was very obscure. It took the first and second floor above a car sales shop. If you wanted a car, it was by appointment only. Jasmin had chosen well; it was quiet and virtually invisible from the street.

There was an internal lounge area and reception with a roof tunnel that lit up the whole area. The hotel reception asked a man to show us to our room. It was up the stairs and then to the right. It was a bit of a rabbit warren that suited our needs.

On opening the door, we had a large room with high wooden beam ceilings with ornate cornicing framing the edges of the room. There was an ensuite bathroom in a cleverly built box with a flat roof in the corner of the room. It was quite a grand room with all the passion of the Italian culture.

Looking out the window, there was a large internal open courtyard five storeys high that bought light into the bedrooms that looked into it. We had a four-poster bed. *This is going to get some use*, I thought.

"Welcome home, baby," Jasmin said in a quiet voice.

I kissed her as we both fell on the bed at the same time. This was as safe as we were going to get. Jasmin started to undress herself and got under the sheets.

"Come on, baby. Let's forget all our troubles. Make love to me. I need you, Mateo."

I got into bed with the love of my life. I wanted to look at her in all her glory. She lay there like a goddess. I was mesmerised by her beauty.

I wanted her so bad. I knew she was looking for love not sex so I took my time with her. It was always love. She was not someone you had sex with. I caressed her body as she was restlessly trying to keep still. She was loving it. She was not just loving, she was sexy to the max.

We made love most of the night. She was at her best. Her body was like a temple and I worshipped it all night.

We needed sleep but it was 5am. We only had four hours left till breakfast at 9am.

We got up for breakfast. Jasmin had a pair of white shorts and a loose T-shirt top on. She was not wearing any underwear.

"Let's go, Mateo," she said as she slipped on her sandals. We meandered our way down the hallways and they widened. There were tables where we would be eating our breakfast in the hallway. There was a nice ambience about it. We could see a small outside area. We said we would sit out there tomorrow. We chattered as we ate our breakfast. My eyes were fixed on Jasmin. I could see the T-shirt showing the shape of her breasts as she moved. Her hair was tied back in a ponytail, that she had bought to her front and it was lying over her breast. Her nipples were standing to attention. They were so long, they stayed in my head. I can't remember what I ate at breakfast. All I could remember was everything about my woman.

My eyes had been transfixed on her for the last hour. As we got up, Jasmin put her arm in mine as we walked back to the room. I must admit I was lost in the hallways. We ended up in the reception area and found our way back from there. We laughed at how we could get lost in a hotel but the reality was we did. Jasmin said she had a contact here and wanted some supplies off of him. She would have to go on her own. I was apprehensive about her going. But she was the man, or should I say the woman. She knew how to look after herself.

She got dressed in the bathroom and as she came out, she put her hair up. She had jeans on and a short sleeve baggy shirt and a baseball cap. She looked like a boy; this was another side of her I had not seen. Jasmin said she would see me later, kissed me and disappeared down the stairs into the street.

I asked the waiter for some coffee; I could see a newspaper in English and some croissants on the reception table so I sat down and had one with my coffee. I was thinking how long would it be before Jasmin returned.

Chapter 18

Mateo

Jasmin arrived back.

"Hello, baby. I'm back." She had a parcel wrapped up. I did not enquire what was in it. I asked for a coffee for her from the reception as I could see she needed one. It appeared like she had been running and slightly out of breath. She settled down into the bucket style chair.

"How did it go, baby? Did you get what you went for?" I asked.

"Yes," Jasmin replied, "I got what was available at short notice."

I said no more. I could only guess what she might have in that parcel. She said no more about it and neither did I. My love was back safe. That was all I wanted to know.

"Shall we go out for lunch?" Jasmin asked.

"Yes," I replied, "I know a nice restaurant near the Milano Cathedral. It's really nice."

"Wow," Jasmin said, "You have been around a lot of places."

"This is my father's country so I have seen a lot of places."

"Let's go then," Jasmin said. "I'm hungry. I've had a busy morning."

We exited the hotel and started walking towards the cathedral. As we walked, a car seemed to be following us. Jasmin looked around at the car. There was a woman driving and a man at the side of her. We could not see in the rear as the windows were tinted black. As they passed us, the woman driver pointed up to a building to the male passenger like she was showing him the area, like a tour guide. I could see Jasmin making a mental note of it.

"The restaurant is over there," I said, pointing.

"Good. Let's go and eat."

The restaurant was busy and we had to wait so we sat at an outside table on the terrazzo. We ordered a bottle of wine. It arrived as the waiter called us in.

"Your table is ready, sir."

We made our way into the dining area; Jasmin scoured the restaurant. We had been given a table near the window. Jasmin spent time looking out in the street. She was looking to see if there was any trouble.

"Jasmin, let's order and chill out. Put everything behind us for now."

"Okay, Mateo. I'm just doing what I do best: looking out for us."

"I love you so much, Jasmin."

She smiled and said, "I love you more."

"You have my words, baby," I laughed. "That's my line."

"Let's share it, my love, for now."

We sat down eating and chatting for hours. Two bottles of wine later, it was time to go. We decided to go and have a look around the cathedral. It was so beautiful. How could man build so many wonderful things then destroy them with wars and neglect? Jasmin was so intrigued with the aesthetics of the cathedral.

"They knew how to build in those days, Mateo."

"Yes," I said, "They did. They started to build it in the early 1300s. It's the second largest in the world."

"It's stunningly beautiful," Jasmin said, "It's so architecturally stunning. I am so glad I've seen it. How do they keep it in such good condition?"

"Full-time maintenance and skilled craftsmen that lovingly restore and maintain it."

"Mateo, we are in Milano and have all these designer shops. Can we go in some? Just perusing."

"I will go along with that but remember we only have small cases."

"I am sure I will find some space in there," she laughed.

We got into the main shopping area. There were models modelling winter clothes outside the shop.

"Let's stay and look at the outfits," she said.

"Okay," I replied, "But we don't want to stay out too long. I feel a bit exposed out here. I'm not sure who is watching us."

"I only want a peep," Jasmin said, "After all, I'm a woman and I have to look good for my man."

After the show, we had a steady walk back to the hotel with Jasmin stopping at all the clothes shops just to peruse the new fashion.

"I want to come back here when all this trouble is sorted. I love new clothes; I feel good in them."

I held her hand and said, "You look wonderful whatever you wear. You make clothes look good. You have the looks and figure most ladies would die to have."

"Thank you, darling. You are too kind. Every woman is beautiful in her own way."

"Yes, I agree," I replied, "Beauty is in the eye of the beholder. I'm with you and you are my princess and I love you for it."

"I love you more, my prince," Jasmin replied.

We made it back to the hotel after what seemed like eighty-five shop stops for Jasmin to feast her eyes. We looked around the streets before going into the hotel so as not to give our secret refuge away to any mercenaries waiting to get rich on our liberty.

We meandered our way back to our room through the hotel corridors. As we opened the door, Jasmin said, "There are some beautiful flowers in the room."

"Wow, you must have an admirer," I said.

"Nobody I know around here, my darling; it must be a present from the hotel."

"No, my love. A present from me for my princess."

Jasmin's eyes welled up with tears of joy.

"Mateo, you are an extraordinary man. You are one of a kind. I'm so glad we are a couple. I hope we are together forever; I could never imagine myself with any other man. Fate bought us together and I will not be the one to break the hand of fate. I hope you feel the same way."

"Yes, I do with all my heart," I replied. "You are the best thing that ever happened to me, even death will not part the love we have for each other."

Jasmin kissed me and asked me to make love to her in this beautiful room. She wanted to remember the moment.

"Give me a minute to change. I want to look special," she said.

"Yes, my darling."

Jasmin came out of the bathroom wearing the sexiest underwear I had ever seen. She was wearing a gold lace bodice with a matching thong. It looked perfect on her and made her look so stunningly sexy. Jasmin walked around the room like she was in an erotic movie. She came and got in bed. Wow, this woman was like a goddess. She was something else.

She was stunningly beautiful and she seemed to glide under the sheets in a silent motion. Her long legs wrapped around mine as she entered the bed. Her body caressed me as she moved, touching all my sensors sending them into high alert knowing love was coming.

I was not aware of the complexity of my woman. She was at another level. Every time we made love, it was a different experience, never the same. After all, what would you expect from a goddess? Only the best. We made love all night. How could I keep up with a goddess of love with an insatiable appetite for her man? I had to meet the benchmark of love we had set and she was surpassing it. The more I loved her, the more she wanted. The night came and went fast and we woke up late. The maid was at the door wanting to make up the room. Jasmin opened the door and asked her to come back in thirty minutes.

Jasmin came back to bed and said, "We have ten minutes and twenty minutes to get ready. Let's use the ten minutes in the best way we can."

She was very attentive and I was receptive. It was the best ten minutes I had ever known. My woman was a dream to behold.

Chapter 19

Mateo

We made our way out of the hotel. It was too late for breakfast so we went to a coffee bar around the corner and had a coffee and panini for brunch. We were trying to make a plan where we would go next. We could not stay in a city too long; it was not safe. Lots of people would be looking for us as there was a price on my head. We decided we would try to head back to France to throw them off our trail.

We would have to get a car, but Jasmin could always find one easily. She was a brilliant car thief. What had we become? But we needed to survive. We agreed to head towards Nice as it was a big city and we could lose ourselves there. We stayed out most of the day looking around shops and sightseeing. We kept out of the main tourist areas.

It was getting late. We could see the sun dropping over the horizon. We walked down the side street back towards the hotel. Jasmin stopped to look at a wedding dress in a wedding shop window. She was discussing how she wanted to get married.

All of a sudden, I looked around to see a car driven by a woman. Two men got out and grabbed me by my arms, trying to pull me into the car. It all happened so fast I was struggling to fend them off. As the car was moving off, they were still trying to get me in to the back seat.

Jasmin had seen it. She leapt forwards opening the front passenger door. She lunged at the woman driver to stop the car and punched her in the face several times. The car crashed into the corner of the building; I was fighting hard with the men in the rear. Jasmin jumped out of the front. She had a large Rambo style commando knife, which she had taken out of her bag. She meant business.

She turned to one of the men outside the car and stabbed the knife in the side of his neck. Pulling it out, he fell to the ground. He had to hold his throat as blood was pouring out of his jugular. I was still fighting the man in the car; Jasmin could see I was in trouble. The man I was fighting was the marine Jasmin had worked with in New York.

She ran behind the car, opened the door and put her fingers into his eyes in a jabbing motion. This man was deadly. She needed to terminate him but wanted to know how much they knew about me and how many more were coming. She stabbed him in the chest, and he cried out.

Jasmin jumped on top of him over the back seat and said, "How many of you are here and why did you come, you bastard?"

He never spoke, just spat at her then said he needed the money. Jasmin pushed his head back and stuck the knife through his throat upwards towards his brain.

"It's no good to you now. You won't be spending anything. You won't need money where you are going," she snarled as she dragged him into the street and ran around. "Mateo, are you okay, my darling?"

I was in a daze. It all happened so fast. Jasmin was a demon. Could anybody stand up to her? My mind was racing. What had she done?

"Yes," I said, "I'm okay. Bit of a scratch but I will live."

She went to the driver. She was out of it, slumped over the wheel. Jasmin had knocked her out with the punch. She seemed lifeless as Jasmin pulled her out from behind the steering wheel onto the street.

"Mateo, get into the front. We have a car now."

Jasmin started the engine and reversed the car, passing over the woman's body. She was not stopping for anybody as she raced off up the street. I looked back. All I could see were three bodies lying in the street. My God, what had we done?

I had definitely joined the right side. My adrenaline was pumping. This was action at its best. What a talent for death my woman had.

We parked the car around the corner from the hotel in an underground car park and made our way into the hotel.

"Clean yourself down, Mateo," Jasmin said, "You have blood all over your face. Let's go straight to the hotel cloakroom and clean up before going through reception. We don't want to bring attention to ourselves. We need to look like we had a lovely day sightseeing."

We cleaned up and made our way back to the room. As we were going into the reception area, Jasmin was covered in blood on one side of her clothes. I managed to change sides just before the reception man saw us. We walked by with our arms around each other laughing.

"Good evening," I said to the porter.

"Good evening, sir and madam," he replied, "Did you have a nice day?"

"Oh yes," Jasmin replied, "Very nice. We did everything we needed to do. Thank you."

We turned down the corridor to the room and shut the door and breathed a sigh of relief.

"What a day…" I said to Jasmin.

"It's over, my love," she replied, "Let's go to bed."

We said we would chat in the morning. It was only early evening but we needed to rest. It had been a busy day to say the least. We were leaving tomorrow for France.

"Good night, my darling," Jasmin said.

"Have we come here to sleep?"

"Yes, my love," she replied, "I don't have the energy for a long night and you know me, baby, once I start you will be up most of the night."

I laughed and put my arms around my woman and went to sleep.

Chapter 20

Mateo

We had decided to make our way up to Nice. France would be good as they would not be looking for us from where we left.

"Let's take the coastal road. It will be nice to look at the Amalfi coastline. I loved Sorrento and Capri was one of my favourite places. What's Nice like, Mateo?"

"It's lovely. Would you like to call at Monaco on the way?"

"Yes please," Jasmin replied.

We were on our way. I was hoping we had put all the past behind us and left everybody chasing us in Italy. Jasmin looked at me.

"My love, you are the best ever." Jasmin held my hand all the way to Monaco never letting go. My woman had melted into her loving self, action woman was gone. At least for the present and I was enjoying having her back. Her eyes seemed to take in all the landscape it encompassed. Jasmin loved Italy. It was her passion and her dream to live there one day.

Jasmin's legs looked so long as she turned rubbing them over my legs. She was out to tease me.

"I want you, Mateo. More than you will ever know. Can we stop and have a look at the views?"

"No, Jasmin," I laughed. "I know why you want to stop and it will make us late getting into Monaco."

"What's it like in Monaco, baby?"

"It's only small but it's one of the most expensive places to live in the world. It's a principality."

"What does that mean, Mateo?"

"It means that the prince of Monaco is the ruler of the principality. He has to make sure there is always one heir to take over the throne or it will revert back to its original origin as there will be no royal blood to take over."

"Wow. So, you mean he has to have lots of children to keep his home?"

"Yes, Jasmin," I said, "One man's meat is one man's poison."

Jasmin punched me in the arm.

"You are mean sometimes, Mateo. It makes me wonder why I fell in love with you," she said, laughing. "I'm only joking. You know I will love you forever."

Jasmin had her eyes out as normal, feasting on everything. Her beautiful eyes took it all in. She was in her element. This was where Jasmin would fit in perfectly. She knew how to mix in the right company and these were her type of people: rich.

"There are lots of up-market properties here, Mateo."

"Yes, my darling. All of them worth tens of millions."

"We might have to wait till next year then," she said, smiling, "When I have sold you, my love."

I looked up and said, "Really, Jasmin? So, you would sell me after all for the right money?"

"Not likely, Mateo. You are not getting off that easy. You are mine for life now. You are not going to be able to wriggle off the line I caught you on."

"You are a darling, Jasmin. *My* darling. Where would I be without you? Can't you see you complete me and make me a better man?"

"You are really kind, my love," Jasmin replied, kissing me on the cheek. I could see Monaco as we rounded the coastal road.

"Look at the views, we are really high up. I can see for miles."

"It looks so nice here. Are we staying for a while?" she asked.

"Yes," I replied, "I will show you around. We have to leave the car somewhere before they trace us. We will leave it outside the city and walk in. We can take the train to Nice. It's all walkable so I will show you around. You will love it here. Keep your purse closed, it will be empty in seconds."

"Wow," Jasmin said, "Is there a lot of crime here?"

"If you call expensive prices in the shops 'robbery', then you are probably right. No, crime is virtually non-existent here. The price to live here is definitely daylight robbery but it's all about supply and demand. The supply is limited so the price is high. If you want a home here, you have to dig deep. There are no short arms and long pockets here, Jasmin. Money goes around fast. You blink and it's gone. Let's find somewhere to stay and we will go out for a look around and catch a bite to eat. I'm hungry."

"So am I, Mateo," she said grabbing me in an inappropriate place.

"Later. Not here," I cried.

Chapter 21

Mateo

We found a small hotel on the French border and freshened up before going out. The sun was hot. Jasmin was wearing tight primrose shorts. Her legs seemed to complement all the clothes she wore like they were all made directly for her. Her curves were out there for all of Monaco to see. She was not wearing any designer clothes; Jasmin made all her clothes look like designer ones. It was Jasmin who got all the attention whilst every other woman was fighting for second place.

We entered the square.

"This is what they call Casino Square, Jasmin. The Hotel de Paris is to the right of us. Look, it shows opulence and wealth."

"Let's go in and have a look at how the really wealthy people live, baby," Jasmin said, linking into my arm.

We looked into the reception, and a door man approached Jasmin.

"Good morning, my lady. Can I help you?"

"Yes, I was thinking about booking a room for a month next year. Do you rent monthly?"

"I would think so," the door man said. "Would you like to see one of our receptionists?"

"No, thank you. I will ask my manager to book it."

We virtually ran out of the door.

Jasmin said, "It is too formal for me. I will stay with the Prince of Monaco instead."

I laughed and said, "Dreamer. Come on, baby, let's go and have a drink in the Café de Paris across the square."

We found a table close to the pavement edge.

"I would like to sit here, darling. Here we can people watch; it will be fun," said Jasmin. "Wow, there are lots of nice cars here. Look, there are Rolls Royces, Ferraris and Lamborghinis. There's every car I dream of owning one day. Can I have one, Mateo?"

"Yes, of course, my sweet. Anything that's mine is yours to share. I will have a look for my keys. Mine is the red Ferrari over there. Not!"

The waiter came over and we ordered two cappuccinos, one each and an extra iced tea for Jasmin. She said she had missed them and had not had one since leaving America. We sat looking at all the well to do people.

Jasmin said, "They're all trying to sit higher than the next person. Why can't everybody be normal and just accept we are all the same? It's just some people have more than others."

"Wow, that's rich coming from you, Jasmin. Look at you. All these are fighting to look like you."

Jasmin laughed, "I never look at myself like that, my love. I'm just me."

"You are a beautiful woman, Jasmin; you are as nice on the inside as the outside."

"Thank you, my darling. You are so kind." Jasmin was looking at the couple on the next table double spooning a large sundae. "That looks really yummy. Can we have one with two spoons so we can share? I want the same as they have got. It looks like you could eat it."

"We are going to eat, my baby."

"I can't wait," Jasmin replied. "I've never seen an ice cream looking so good."

The waiter bought over the sundae; Jasmin's eyes opened wide. I looked across the table. Her eyes were drawing me in like a whirlpool in a river. I was spinning around hopelessly out of control.

Was I going to be able to swim out or was it going to drag me down into it? My eyes were spinning with her beauty. I was definitely being drawn in and had been since the day on the train when we met. My mind was just ticking on overtime as I was looking at my woman. She was everything I could ever want.

I looked around the tables. It seemed all eyes were on us. I couldn't say it was the attention we were looking for at the moment. We ate the sundae really slowly; it was too nice to eat fast. We wanted it to last. It was what I wanted for us: to last a lifetime and never grow out of love. Jasmin was loving it all.

"Mateo, thank you for bringing me here. I love it. I could sit here all day. The sun is lovely and hot. I wish I had bought my bikini with me."

"That would have opened some eyes," I joked.

"It's all for you, Mateo. You know, don't you?"

"Yes, my darling Jasmin, you are my lover. I must be the luckiest man on Earth."

"Well, I must be the luckiest woman on Earth then."

We agreed to disagree and held each other's hand.

"There is something missing on your left hand," I said.

Jasmin looked in horror.

"A wedding ring," I added.

Jasmin smiled and said, "Don't ask. Let's go straight to the altar. I'm yours."

"Soon, my love. When the time is right."

Jasmin looked across the square and pointed to the Monte Carlo Casino.

"Can we go there tonight, my love? I would love to go there; we can get dressed up and look like millionaires."

"Look like millionaires? Yes, we will definitely shock them all," I replied.

We left the Café de Paris.

"Let's go to see the Japanese garden," I suggested.

"I feel at home here walking around the streets," Jasmin replied.

We walked between the high buildings fronting the streets. As we walked, we could see the sun was shining between the buildings. As it shone through the buildings, it caught Jasmin's hair. It was shimmering from the sun rays and it lit up her body like a beacon of light. Showing the way for ships at sea. She was glowing. She smiled. This was my woman. As we walked, I felt a warm embrace of Jasmin's arms and a kiss

"I love you, my Mateo."

"I love you more, my beautiful Jasmin."

We arrived at the Japanese garden. It was only a small, ponded garden but there was a feeling of calm and tranquillity. It had a heavenly aura about it, so peaceful. Jasmin was enjoying every moment being there. It was like an oasis in a desert. The concrete buildings of Monaco around us being the desert. We sat down and chattered about all the best things we wanted to do in our lives. Looking over the water watching the male dragonflies dancing over the water looking to mate before the end of the season, to ensure his future family.

"I want you to be like him, Mateo. I want us to mate and leave a family behind us. I don't want our bloodline to end. I want us to be remembered by our children and their children. I can't think of anything I want more than that."

"I will make it all happen, my love."

Jasmin turned to me and kissed me like never before.

"Thank you, darling, thank you. I will love you forever," Jasmin said.

I was still coming up for air when I cleared my voice and said, "I will love you forever as well, my baby."

That was the best kiss ever, I thought. What a woman.

We walked through the narrow streets. They were busy and we had to avoid the cars.

"Keep close, darling," I said. She was so close. There was no room for a blade of grass between us. She was holding me that tight. "You will be able to see the prince's palace soon. It's around the corner."

Chapter 22

Mateo

"There it is, my love. Let me show you around the prince's palace," I said.

"I'm looking forward to that," Jasmin said.

We walked into the grounds of the palace.

Jasmin said, "Who can afford to live in this palace here in Monaco?"

"Prince Albert."

"I would like to live here with you as a prince and me as your princess. Just think, my darling, we could have parties every week and fancy balls. I could look like the fairy princess and you could be the handsome prince. Am I dreaming, Mateo?"

"Possibly, my love. That only happens in films."

We went into the palace.

"It's beautiful in here, darling. Look at these ceilings and walls. The whole room oozes opulence and wealth. I love this way of living; do you think they are happy living here, baby?"

"Not sure, my love, not necessarily. There is always some tragedy that happens, like Princess Grace who lived here was killed in a car crash and Princess Diana died in a car crash. So, life is precious and we should look after it. Having wealth and happiness don't always go hand in hand."

We spent two hours perusing the whole palace and Jasmin never stopped asking questions. She was so interested in this way of life.

We decided to go back to the hotel and have some chill time before going to the casino. Jasmin was excited about going.

"I've never been to a casino and you are taking me to one of the best in the world. I can't wait to see inside and how you can win money there."

"Not everyone wins, my love."

"Mateo, you are very cynical today. Princesses in car crashes and people losing money… Let's move forward and be more positive. We will have to set a limit on our money and not go beyond it. We cannot afford to be using cards as we can be traced," Jasmin said. "I'm going to have a relaxing bath, my love. You are welcome to join me."

"I would love to but I need to sort some things out before we go out. I need to work out a strategy on how we can win tonight."

Jasmin filled the bath, undressed and stepped into the bath. I looked at her. *Forget the strategy. I'm going in the bath with Jasmin*, I thought.

"Whatever happened to your strategy, darling," she said while grabbing my manhood as I stepped in to join her. All I remember was there was lots of splashing. The bath was getting hotter and hotter. Jasmin fuelling the heat. She was red hot.

That was the best bath of my life.

Chapter 23

Jasmin

We got out and dried each other. What an experience that was.

I stood there whilst Mateo took his time drying every inch of my body. I was excited by the personal attention I was receiving. I told him my heart was racing and I wanted him to make love to me before we went out. We pulled the bedsheets back.

"Silk sheets, Mateo. Let's slide in between them and make love, my darling." I was hungry for him. "I want all of you, Mateo. Hold nothing back!"

I bet he thought winning my love was like being the king of the Achaeans and being handed the keys to the gates of Troy. I was challenging him to win. The gates were open; he was going to do his best to meet the target I had set.

I was unusually quiet this evening. I was enjoying the love too much to be vocal.

"I surrender to you, my lover. You are the best."

Thoughts crossed my mind as I lay there. Mateo did not look like a Greek god, but he was toned in all the right places. His skin was not what you would expect from a half-Italian man. It was smooth and smelt sweet, not sweaty like men before. His touch was gentle and caressing, like warm water running over your body. He was passionate, not leaving one area of my body untouched. He left me with a feeling of satisfaction that he had done everything to make all my senses stand to attention and enjoy the moment. He never rushed and made sure I had complete fulfilment, that I had been there and experienced love like I had never known before. I loved him so much. He was my man; my one and only. A man you search for but never find, like a ghost that does not exist, but you feel his presence in your dreams. A man you could only dream about, knowing his name: a gift from the gods. He turned me on so much.

Chapter 24

Mateo

I got out of bed a better man than I went in. Jasmin had surrendered her love to me to look after. I wondered if the task was too much to be intrusted to myself. I had never been somebody that a person would have openly put their trust into, never mind a goddess like Jasmin. I felt really appreciated and loved.

We were ready and walked a short way to Casino Square. It was bustling with lots of people sitting outside the Café de Paris, mingling with each other trying to get the last twilight hours out of the day. It was early evening and we could see the sun shining for the last hour through the clouds like a light show from a laser, beaming light in rays behind the Hotel de Paris. It looked fabulous.

Jasmin was excited she was going to bet at one of the world's most famous casinos. We had pre-signed in during the day so we were good to go. We had set our exit money to two hundred and fifty euros. We could not afford to lose more than that. It was our limit.

We started to look around at the roulette, blackjack and poker tables and the machines. Jasmin wanted to play on the machines so I gave her fifty euros. She was putting it in like there was going to be no tomorrow. I was panicking. We would be out of here in ten minutes. I was thinking at least three hours of fun, but she was playing three machines at once. How was she keeping all three going? This was a lady that had never been in a casino? She got through forty euros with ten euros left. On the next pull, one of the machines flashed. She had won six thousand euros. Two minutes later, another flashed for four thousand euros. She had won ten thousand euros with forty euros. People were starting to look over at us, the lucky couple.

"Not too bad for a beginner," she said.

I was a bit stunned by it all. Was it skill or just luck? She must have caught them just right, as they were programmed to only pay out jackpots every blue moon. I said it was the luck of the draw.

"Just a spell of beginner's luck," Jasmin said. "I confused the machines the way I played them."

"Jasmin, there is only one thing confused and it's not the machines."

She was on a winning streak and had over ten thousand euros to spend. She was on a roll and wanted to ride with it.

"Let's go into where the gambling tables are, baby," she said. Jasmin was running around and I was just following her. She was orchestrating the night. It was no longer my shout; she was running the show now.

"Mateo, I need some chips, please, to bet on the roulette table."

Did she know what she was doing? How would she know the table rules? She was racing to put on bets, she was miles ahead of me. I was trying to catch my breath. I came over and she had put a bet on black with evens as the odds and the ball was rolling around the wheel. It rolled over the wheel in what seemed like slow motion, waiting for it to land in one of the numbers: fifteen black.

Jasmin roared, "Yes, yes, yes."

Was it beginner's luck? I was starting to question whether or not Jasmin had been in a casino before and knew all the angles and tricks. Was it purely luck? There was no skill, I told myself, with black and red evens. With just a spin of the wheel, she had doubled her money.

We were the new kids on the block with luck on our side. We were on a winning streak and cleaning up. Never in the big league but nevertheless getting richer by the minute. This couldn't last as we knew the house always won. If we had won and could walk out with our stake, we would have had a good night out on the casino royale.

Jasmin was still on the roulette table; she was placing bets everywhere. I think she was just edging her bets. The croupier spun the wheel fast and the ball was flying around the wheel above, trying to find a place to land. Like a paratrooper trying to miss the trees, the ball seemed like it was never going to land.

All of a sudden, he called out, "Thirty-five."

"That's me," Jasmin cried out, "It's me, it's me! I've won big, my darling. I've got it all."

The croupier put the chips on the table that she had won. It was a good-sized stack.

"It's time to go. We need to leave. Let's cash the chips in," I said.

"Just a few more, my darling."

"We are attracting too much attention."

She suddenly came to her senses and said, "Okay, Mateo, let's go."

We cashed in the chips for cash and exited the casino. We had around twenty-eight thousand euros in cash. I had ten thousand and Jasmin kept eighteen thousand euros.

As we rounded the corner behind the Hotel de Paris near the shops, Jasmin said, "Can we look over at the views of the harbour?"

I was apprehensive as we were carrying a lot of money but I thought why not. We went to the wall and looked into the harbour. We were looking at all the super yachts when we noticed two men approaching us. Jasmin kicked off her high heels.

"We have trouble here, Mateo."

The two men spoke Russian.

"They want the money that we have won," she said.

"What did you tell them, Jasmin?" I asked.

"I've told them to get back to Russia. They are not getting it."

The two men ran towards us. Jasmin side stepped one of them and she punched him in the kidneys as he ran by and knocked him into the wall.

"Watch out, Mateo," Jasmin said as the other man was running towards me. I dropped to the floor quickly as he lunged forwards, tripping over me. He hit his head on the wall. He was dazed and not in a good way. Jasmin saw him getting up. She ran at him and dropped kicked him in the back. It was so powerful; he virtually flew over the wall and down the cliff. The other man was still trying to recover from the punch in the kidney.

She grabbed him by his hair and pulled him across the patio to the wall. She pulled him up and showed him the drop. He had a gun that Jasmin relived him of. Jasmin put the gun to his head hard.

"Who are you working for?"

"No one," he said. He saw us win the money and thought it could change hands to his. Jasmin was pressing on his head with her bare foot. She emptied the gun magazine of bullets and threw the gun into the harbour.

In Russian, she said, "Do you want to join him?"

The man put one hand in the air. He was not ready to go over the wall. Jasmin punched him in the face and knocked him clean out. They wouldn't be robbing again soon. I asked Jasmin if she was okay.

"Never better," she replied.

My woman fought like a man; she showed no mercy to anybody. I thought I better not stray with this woman, I'm not sure how she would react. Strangely, I felt proud to have her on my arm even though she was a true widow maker. This was Malak the Destroyer at her best.

We went back to the hotel and Jasmin was hot. Nothing to do with the fight but terminating an evil person seemed to turn her on and she wanted to make love. She was removing my clothes as the room door shut. She was melting and I needed to satisfy her insatiable appetite. I was food and she was starving. She was going to feast on me. I must confess my mind was on the Russian caved in on the rocks below the casino. Jasmin just wanted loving and I could make no excuses, as she looked sexy as hell.

Chapter 25

Mateo

Of all the men in the world, why had she fallen in love with me? She would have men falling at her feet. I looked at her sleeping. She was at peace. Nobody was going to scare my woman. She was Malak the Destroyer, but looked like an angel sent by God to rescue me as she slept. She had a peaceful night.

My mind was racing. I could not sleep so I lay there looking at her most of the night. I thought about the people we had terminated. How different their lives may have been if they had not been mercenaries or thieves. I had to think what I could do. I might be able to phone the UK and give myself up and they might not imprison me for breaking the Official Secrets Act, my confidentiality agreement and trying to defect and sell information about the weapon system I had been instrumental in inventing. I didn't think anybody would ever trust me again. Could it be they would pick me and Jasmin up and fly us back to the UK?

Jasmin started to wake up.

"Good morning, darling," she said. "I had a lovely sleep. Come here, my love. I want a hug please."

I put my arms around her and gently squeezed her. I could feel her hot against my body. I felt myself going to sleep. I had not had a wink of sleep all night but Jasmin was awake and needed some attention.

We went out for breakfast; it was nice to sit outside in the morning sun. We chattered but I held back on my thoughts of last night.

"Where are we going today, my love?" Jasmin asked.

"I think we will take a walk to the harbour. There are some nice restaurants down there. We can have lunch there later and look at the boats coming in."

"That will be nice," Jasmin replied.

"Let's go into Nice tomorrow. I will book a hotel and tonight can be our last night here."

"I'm good to go wherever you want, my love."

"Great. I will book it, baby, and we can leave after breakfast. Let's enjoy the day."

We made our way down towards the harbour area. We could see a chalked outline of the body of the Russian thief that the police forensics had marked out to investigate. The body had gone and we could see police asking the business owners nearby if they had seen anything.

We hurried beyond the crime scene into the harbour. We sat outside and had a coffee; it was so pleasant there it seemed nothing was too much trouble. They made us feel so welcome. We spent a few hours there; we drank a few beers and a bottle of wine. It was a great place.

I looked over at Jasmin who looked good enough to eat. I thought I would save that thought until later.

"Do they have Formula One races here and where is the track?" she asked.

"You are nearly on it."

"Where?" she said, "I can't see it."

"No, you can't. Once a year, most of the roads in Monaco are turned into a Formula One racetrack and barriers are erected everywhere. The whole of Monaco comes out to watch the race. It's one of the richest races out of all of them. You can see them going through the tunnel there so fast and loud you need ear defenders on."

"Wow," Jasmin said, "I would love to see the race here one day, baby."

"I will bring you," I replied.

"I will hold you to that, my love," Jasmin said.

"Definitely."

"Let's go back to the hotel," she said.

I agreed and decided to make our way back for a lie down to relax. I thought whatever floated Jasmin's boat,

I'm good for. After all, she was the master of the ship. There wasn't going to be a munity in our relationship.

We got into the room and Jasmin wanted control of everything.

"I want you, Mateo. I was looking at you in the restaurant coming back from the toilets. I had you in my sights as you walked back to me. I could see an outline of parts of you sticking out. It turned me on. I couldn't stop thinking about it until I had you. I think you need to put those tight shorts away; they are too revealing. I want to be on top to give you the ride of your life, my darling."

"I can go for that, my love. That will be different and I am sure I will enjoy it."

"Just lie there, my darling, and I will make it all happen for you. Relax, I'm all yours."

Jasmin was wild. I felt the heavens had opened and swallowed me in a moment of ecstasy. My woman knew all the right buttons and she was pressing them all. What an afternoon. I was not sure if we would make dinner out, so I phoned down to reception and booked an evening meal in the hotel.

Chapter 26

Mateo

The morning came round fast and we were on our way around the mountain towards Nice. The views of the bay were really stunning. We navigated the winding mountain roads passing all the small bays with racing yachts in the water, waiting to start a race like greyhounds in a trap waiting for the hare to pass and the traps to open. The drive was an epic look into a picture postcard.

We started down the road into Nice. We could see all the harbour and its amazing diversity of floating luxury yachts. Driving around the peninsula of the harbour, we joined the Promenade de Anglaise. It was a three-lane motorway running along the beach all the way down to the airport. We had booked into the Palais de la Méditerranée halfway down facing the sea. It was a fairly new hotel with a colonial style facade. The one problem we encountered: it had a casino below. This was not a good thing although Jasmin was a wizard with the games. This was not somewhere to go after our altercation in

Monaco. We would have to bypass the temptation to go down and gamble.

We signed in and the room was ours for three nights. I thought we could do a bit of sightseeing. We had a room with a sea view. We could see through the pillars of the façade; it was a framed picture of the Mediterranean. A one-shot photo of the Cote d'Azur. The French Riviera.

We laid on the bed. It was nice to feel the air conditioning cooling the room. It had been hot in the midday sun. Jasmin said she was hot and took all her clothes off and lay on the bed. My eyes had come away from looking out the window at a beautiful view to looking at my woman spread across the bed.

Jasmin was the best view on the Cote d'Azur and I had a box seat. The best seat in the house having the show of my life. She lay there with her long silky hair parting either side of her nipples. It was cool in the room and she was responding to the change in temperature with her body. They seemed to be moving the hair lying on her perked breasts. She moved onto her front facing the window, showing her curves as the sun shone through the window. Her body looked sun-kissed and felt like satin as I rubbed my hands across it.

"That's lovely, darling," she whispered, "Please massage me more. I love you touching me. You have strong hands, my love."

I could not stop myself going further and we ended the afternoon in a passionate embrace of love and lust.

We showered together before going out. We washed each other. I had never seen so much soap in the shower. It was the best shower ever. My personal areas seemed like they had been washed beyond redemption. Would they ever feel normal again? I hoped not.

Jasmin was one of a kind; the best at everything she did. If you were in a relationship with her, she worshipped you, but if you were on her bad side that would be a dangerous move. There would be no stone unturned until she found you and terminated your miserable life.

We got dressed ready to go out.

"Are we going somewhere nice, my darling?" she asked.

"Yes, I'm going to take you to a nice fish restaurant. They have fresh lobster in tanks. You can pick one and they will cook it fresh for you."

"That sounds lovely," Jasmin said. "Do they kill it first?"

"No, baby, they put it in boiling water that kills it."

"Hmmm, that sounds cruel, darling."

"It's no worse than being caught on a line or in a net. You just don't have to think about it. Just enjoy the moment."

"Can I really choose my own?"

"Yes, my love. Any one you want."

Jasmin chose the one with dark markings on the claws.

"That one there, darling. It looks nice."

The waiter removed it from the tank and took it to the kitchen to cook it.

Jasmin said, "I would like it all please."

"You're welcome to it. Enjoy, my love. You deserve it," I replied.

Jasmin was tucking into the lobster. There was nothing left but shell. She had been in every claw, nook and cranny to find every last bit of meat.

"What a lobster," she said, "I'm full. I've never had anything so tasty in my life, my love. Where do you think they caught it?"

"I think they caught it in the Aegean Sea. Achilles caught it himself and brought it here."

"Really?" she cried.

I could not stop laughing.

"If he had, it would not have tasted that good as it would have been three thousand years old."

Jasmin grabbed me by the private parts and said, "That's not funny, is it?"

"No, my love. Be careful with something we both share. Nobody wants damaged goods."

Jasmin released her grip and we both laughed.

"I almost believed you but it did taste lovely. I'm glad you bought me here, I've had a really good time. I have loved every minute of it."

We finished the wine and the waiter bought us two liquors over.

"These are on the house," he said.

I did not want one. I was on my limit for drink. Jasmin took them both.

"Down the hatch," she said, polishing one after the other. I looked in horror. She could drink me under the table all day every day. Jasmin had probably spent time in bars with men from her regiment between missions. She could fight like a man so I had no reason to think she could not drink like one.

Jasmin and I had a walk around the square. It was still warm and the moon was full, lighting up the dark sky. As we walked back along the promenade, the sea was restless with the waves crashing on the beach in a white-water show. The air off the sea filled our lungs with oxygen driving out the stale air from the traffic on the road. We felt alive, the oxygen had bought us a surge of energy.

Jasmin said, "Can we sit on the beach under the stars?"

I looked at her eyes. She wanted to be close to me. I could see she had possibly been thinking about us and I could see she was worried. Her mind was wrestling with the fact she could lose me. We sat down on the beach. She cuddled up to me and kissed me.

171

"We will always be together. God willed it; I too am a gift from God. It's in my name. Like yours, my love. We were meant to be. God brought us together and I know now no man can separate us. You're mine for eternity."

As Jasmin kissed me, it strangely felt final like she knew something was going to happen.

"Let's walk," she said. She was picking up stones from the beach and throwing them into the sea like it was a big wishing well.

I held her hand. I could see her eyes welling up with tears. She looked like a lost soul searching for somebody to help her out of the pain she was feeling. In her thoughts, I could see her talking under her breath. Her hand gripped mine like she was holding on to me for dear life the best way she could. She was between here and somewhere else. She turned to me. Tears were rolling down her face; her eyes were like waterfalls full of water.

"Don't leave me, Mateo," she cried. "I don't want you to go anywhere."

I hugged her and assured her I was not going anywhere and that I would always be here for her. She was sobbing uncontrollably.

"You are my life," she sobbed, "I would not want to live without you. It was fate when we met and it will be fate when we die. I'm yours now and nothing else matters but me and you. I love you unlimited with no barriers. They are all down for you." She seemed to regain control of her emotions and wiped her eyes. "Sorry for being silly and crying, but I love you more than life itself and I am emotional around you sometimes. Forgive me."

"There is no need for forgiveness," I said, "I love you so much as well. I will always be your man. I have the best woman ever, a true angel sent from God." I felt like the most privileged man on Earth to have such a beautiful woman who loved me unlimited.

We had a fairly long way still to walk.

"Let's walk along the road and see if we can catch a taxi back to the hotel," I said.

"Yes, my love, that would be nice."

We managed to get one and arrived at the hotel. We went to bed and I put my arms around her in bed as we both fell asleep.

Chapter 27

Mateo

I woke up. It was morning. We had slept in exactly the same position as we went to bed. My arm ached slightly as Jasmin had been sleeping on it all night. I managed to pull it out from underneath her without waking her up. I sat at the bottom of the bed looking at her sleep. She looked like an angel but this was Malak the Destroyer lying there. A true widow maker. A terminator.

I went to the bathroom to have a wash and clean my teeth. Jasmin had woken up and had come into the bathroom to use the toilet. She was nude and looked yummy as she sat there. She stood up; her breasts poking out like they were on invisible wires. Her body looked like it had been sculpted by Michelangelo depicting Aphrodite the Greek goddess of love and beauty. She had everything: the body, the beauty, and the personality all rolled together.

My princess was ready for the day and hungry.

"Can we go down for breakfast, my love? I'm going to massacre the buffet today. I'm starving," she said.

We ate well. Jasmin had everything, including two bowls of fruit. She said she was bought up on it and enjoyed it every day. She had eaten like she was not going to eat again for a while.

We went back to the room to get ready; Jasmin had put on some jeans and a black t-shirt and tied her hair back into a ponytail and she had her gym trainers on. I looked at her. Although really pretty, this was not how Jasmin usually dressed. I wondered if she was expecting trouble. Was her sixth sense telling her something?

We went into the foyer and Jasmin had a look at the newspapers in the stand. She noticed a small picture of me on the fifth page. She put it back.

"We have to go," she said.

We put a step on and walked down the pavement. I was going to show Jasmin around Nice. But now, I needed to find a hat and some mirrored sunglasses to disguise myself. We found a shop in a parallel street and I came out looking fairly obscure. Nobody would notice me now.

"Do you think I am obscure enough to go out?" I asked her.

"Of course. Nobody will recognise you now."

"Okay, we can get on a tour bus and see the city."

"That's a good idea. We won't be noticed too much around other people."

We had a day of sightseeing around Nice.

"It's a large city," Jasmin said.

"Yes, it is. It's the second largest in France. Lots to do here for a lady with lots of time on her hands and a full bank account. It's a vibrant metropolis."

Jasmin caught sight of the designer shops.

"I would like to stop and catch the last hour in the shops, darling, before we go for dinner."

I accepted the impossible and said, "Be careful with the money. We are limited."

"We have lots," Jasmin laughed. "Have you forgot about our winnings?"

I admitted I had a momentary loss of memory.

"Go ahead, babe. Smash it, spend big."

As she made her way into the shop, I told her I would wait outside. I was enjoying breathing sea air coming across the promenade.

"Make sure you're in sight of me as it's not safe anywhere on the continent."

I was looking around. It was that time of night when deliveries were being dispatched from the shops and orders were being delivered. There were a lot of commercial vans and lorries parked outside the shops. I noticed a large unmarked plain black van reversing in between two lorries.

I looked into the shop window and saw Jasmin at the rear of the shop coming out of the changing rooms with some clothes talking to the assistant. I heard the rear door on the van opening. Three Korean-looking men came out. They rushed over.

As I turned around, they grabbed me by the arms and one had his hand in my back pushing me towards the rear of the van. It was all happening so quickly. I looked back towards the shop window. I could see Jasmin was horrified to see them throwing me into the back of the van. I could see her dropping the clothes and running through the shop to the door at lightning speed.

The men were strong and got me into the back of the van quickly. I had no time to fight back. They had taken me completely by surprise. As they forced me into the van, I saw Jasmin running out the door towards the van but the doors slammed and I could see her no more. I was being held down by two of the men. I was in big trouble this time. The van tyres were screeching as they took off. They meant business.

Chapter 28

Jasmin

I had to think quick. If I lost the van, I would lose Mateo. I looked quickly down the street as there were a few cars on the way up the street but I needed a "go anywhere" vehicle to get through the traffic to catch up with the van. As I turned, I heard a motorbike. It was a Scrambler Trial like bike.

I ran into the road and kicked the rider off the bike. I picked up the bike and tore off, tyres smoking in the direction the van was travelling. I could see it far in the distance. I had to catch up as it could go off the promenade onto a side street and disappear at any time. I was dodging in and out of traffic at speed, clipping cars as I raced to catch the van.

I managed to catch up and stayed a pace behind it. I needed to find out where they were taking him. They exited on the costal road back towards Antibes. I was mad with myself for leaving him outside. I should have made him come in. My thoughts were on overtime.

As I sped along, I looked down at the speedometer and saw the petrol. Thank God, it was nearly full. The van started to turn towards the motorway back to Marcia. I kept a good distance. My problem was if the rider of the bike had informed the police. Or if he was still trying to recover and I was okay for a short time. We would be going through tolls on this road and would have to stop. I wondered if I had change or if I could use a card. The van was speeding up and making distance. I had to focus. I opened the bike up and narrowed the gap.

I wondered what state Mateo was in and if he was even alive still. After all, there was a full contract on him dead or alive. The bounty money was more for alive but what worried me was who wanted him dead. The stakes had changed for the worst. As I looked at the van, it started to sway from side to side. Was it Mateo fighting in the van or was it the driver?

Minutes later, it regained its correct line on the road. Whatever had happened had been sorted. I was concerned they had killed him.

The van was exiting the motorway towards the mountain gap of Grenoble. They were possibly going to head towards northern Europe. I followed for twenty-five kilometres and they turned down a farm type track. I had to be careful. It was a dusty road and if they looked back, they might see the dust the bike was kicking up. I held right back just keeping the van in eyesight. It seemed to turn and I could see it going into a yard area and stopping.

As I looked, I saw them dragging Mateo out the van. He was alive. I breathed a sigh of relief. All I had to do now was rescue him. I needed some tools; they were all back at the hotel.

I would have to risk it for ninety minutes both ways to get my weapons from the hotel to fight them. It looked like they were there overnight so I sped back to the hotel. My mind was racing. Had I made a mistake coming back? Would they be leaving or worse transferring him into another vehicle for an ongoing journey?

I rushed back.

Thank you, thank you, I thought, *they are still here*. Now all I had to do was get Mateo with the least collateral damage. There were four men. Mateo could be tied up so I would have to write him out unless I could free him to help me. I needed a diversion to see if I could lower the odds to fifty percent.

I looked and there was an outside light on. I could see three of the kidnappers outside smoking. They were all quite thick set builds; they looked like they all used the gym. They would be strong and I would have to stay clear of hand-to-hand combat unless I had no choice. I needed to shoot them if I could, but ammunition was limited and a fire fight could alert neighbours to the area. I had to plan where the diversion would take place.

Somebody had been doing some cattle fencing and had left a roll of fence wire.

"This will do," I said.

Walking over towards a small wooded area, I tied the wire at around five foot high between two trees, and another two further into the woods. It was dark in the woods, perfect for my trap. I needed to use myself as bait and get them into the woods. *I can handle two of them*, I thought. *If three come, I might be in trouble but I still have a gun so I can kill them all.*

I was set to go. I had to make sure they would come into the woods to investigate the explosion I had planned. I was fully tooled up. I was not going to be easy to defeat. I had a large Rambo knife in the top of my trousers, additional explosives, and a lady's chrome silver pearl-handle gun.

I needed them to follow me into the woods, running at speed. I had to distract them by falling over making the distance between us smaller. When I got up and ran, they would focus on me and not on what might be in the woods. The plan was good. All I had to do was create the diversion and let the rest take its place. My only chance was to split them into twos.

I made my way down to the farmhouse. There was a barn with some disused machinery and tractors. I started to climb onto the tractor to look over at the farmhouse to see if Mateo was close to the entrance. As I pulled myself up, I pulled a shelf down with old water cans on it. They clanked on the way down making a loud noise.

"Shit, I can't believe it."

All the lights went on outside the farmhouse. Two men came running from around the rear of the building. They must have been smoking outside. They were too close to have come out of the house. I turned and started running towards the woods. They were gaining on me. Could I make it to the woods before they caught me? It had not worked out the way I thought it would have. I felt I was in the Olympics running for the USA in the final but the consequences of being caught would be termination not a gold medal.

I entered the woods. They were at top speed behind me. They were virtually on me just touching me trying to grab hold of me, just slipping off my shoulders. As we ran, I dropped to the floor. They both ran over me. I heard the wire twang. I looked up and it had gone halfway through their throats. There was blood pumping out everywhere. They were no longer a threat; their heads were hanging off their shoulders. It had worked but not as I had planned but I was happy with the results.

I said to myself, "Two more scumbags still to sort out."

I ran to the edge of the woods. The two men had come out to see what was happening. They could not see me but I could see them. I pulled my pistol out and picked one off with the first bullet. He fell to the ground.

The other man pulled a gun out and started shooting randomly into the woods. I had already flanked him and was behind the farmhouse. He was still shooting into the woods. I had to risk either taking him out with the gun or the knife. I was short on bullets. He continued to reload his gun and started firing into the woods. I took out the combat knife and threw it into his back that hard it knocked him over. He was out of it. The knife had gone right through him into his chest. As I dragged it out, blood spurted everywhere, all over me. It was the blood of a pig, expendable at zero money.

The man I shot had crawled into the farmhouse. As I opened the door, I could see Mateo tied to a chair. The man was holding a knife next to Mateo's neck, talking in broken Chinese about what he was going to do to Mateo if I didn't put the gun down and surrender.

I put my hands up. Nobody was going to kill my man. He was shouting for me to drop my gun. I did as he said. As I dropped it, it slid down my arm and I caught it as it left my arm. The trigger was cocked ready to fire and it blew a hole in his face as I fired it.

Mateo dropped over in the chair he was tied to. I ran over and stuck the knife in the man's chest to make sure he was dead. Mateo looked in horror. I'm sure he thought I was going to take his scalp. Mateo looked upset that he was so close as I had fired.

"You were never in danger, my love," I reassured him.

Mateo smiled as his face cracked with fear. After all, I was Malak the Destroyer. A true widow maker, a deadly terminator.

Chapter 29

Mateo

None of these men would be returning home for the big pay out. There was not going to be one. We put the bike into the rear of the van. Jasmin said it would be best if we travelled in this from now on.

"I think it's time to leave Nice and head towards the mountains out of the cities. They are not safe," she added.

We drove back to the hotel. It seemed quiet. I was talking about all the people we had killed. Jasmin asked me to put it behind us and not think too much about it.

"They would have killed you," she said, "I've never seen them before but they were bad men and deserved to die a violent death. There was no honour for them where they were going, fire stokers. Let's drive through the night and get some distance between us and Nice, my love."

"Yes, baby," I replied. I had been to the toilet. My stools were loose. She had frightened me more than the kidnappers. I thanked the lord she was on my side. I wasn't sure whether to laugh or cry but I was safe.

"I will drive," she said. "We need to move fast and get out of here. We will make our way up to Gap. We should be there early morning."

I was already under the weather; I obviously did not look well enough to drive. The last thing I wanted was a nightmare drive around the mountain roads. I asked if Jasmin had any large nappies.

"Don't worry, baby," she laughed, "I will take it easy."

I sighed in relief. It might not be so bad. After all, my stomach was on a cliff edge and I could take no more.

She turned to me and asked, "Who do you think has put that kill contract out on you?"

"I'm not sure."

"It must be a high price on your head, my darling. You are famous. Everyone wants a piece of you, Mateo."

We drove into the centre of Gap. Jasmin spotted a bakery and pulled into the car park.

"Let's have some pastries and a coffee for breakfast, my love."

The pastries and bread smelt fabulous; I could smell them before I exited the van.

"You stay here," Jasmin said.

"Yes, okay," I said. "My eyes are closing. I've had a busy twenty-four hours. I will wait for you here."

I looked around the van when I saw a bag. My curious nature allowed me to open the bag. Inside was a full arsenal of grenades, guns, bullets, and a repeater shotgun. Where was Jasmin going to be expecting trouble? She had more hardware in that bag than the battalion's store.

Jasmin had seen two women behind her in the bakery. It looked like she was weighing them up. Even I could tell, they were not local to here. The locals were more like mountain people. These were city girls. I could see they were packing knives and guns. Were they undercover police? I was not sure but I knew they were not in the bakery to buy cakes.

"Buckle up, Mateo. We will eat en route," Jasmin said.

We decided to make our way up towards Grenoble to get some distance as Gap was too close to Nice. Jasmin was tired and wanted to have a break so we pulled over to an open area. She got out and looked over the mountain edge.

"It's a long way down there. We must be around two thousand metres up," she said. "I won't be long, my darling. I will just find a private place."

I could see her marching up the track opposite when a car pulled in front of the van. Two women jumped out and came to the van. I did not know the area. It was no good asking me for directions. I could see one of them had a gun in her hand. The other had some rope. They weren't here for directions.

I tried locking the door as they passed the bonnet, but it was not locking. I panicked to lock it and the woman opened the door and told me to get out in a British voice. They forced me over the seat with a gun to my head and told me to put my hands behind my back. They started tying my hands.

They dragged me up by my arms. They were more like men in their strength and resolve as they shut the door and walked me to the front of the van. Jasmin came from nowhere like a wild animal, knocking me out the way. She did a roundhouse kick to the woman with the gun, knocking her straight over the mountain edge. I could hear her screaming.

As she was going down the mountain, the other woman attacked. The woman was a good fighter and Jasmin had her back to the mountain edge. I was helpless; my hands were tied behind my back. I thought I could kick her or head butt her. I was not in a position to help as they were in a fierce fight.

Jasmin was using her arms, blocking attacks from the woman. She had been instrumental in her friend's death and she wanted blood. Jasmin was still fighting to get away from the cliff edge as she was not fighting in a good place. I ran towards the woman in a violent crash knocking her to the ground. She sprung up like a spring coming out of a mattress. It was that fast, it looked surreal. She fought like she was fully trained in combat. Jasmin saw an opportunity and took it, rushing over and kicking her in the face. She went down backwards away from the edge.

I went over and kicked her in her ribs whilst she was on the ground.

She managed to get up and ran towards Jasmin. As she gathered speed and she went to hit her, Jasmin blocked her and used the momentum of her speed against her. Jasmin dropped down and lifted her up like a ballerina into the air above her head and threw her. She went flying over the mountain edge. The scream was haunting as she went into the ravine below. As we looked over, she was still screaming.

Jasmin shouted, "Say hello to your mate, bitch."

We saw her, in the distance, hit the bottom. Jasmin continued shouting.

"You horrible bitch. Rot in hell." Jasmin untied my hands. "It seems every time you're out of my sight, trouble finds you. You will have to stay in sight of me, my darling, as one day I might not be able to save you."

Jasmin was happy she had seen them coming to the van and had been able to rescue me from them. I think it had made her adrenaline reach boiling point, but afterwards she was ready to make love and she was hot for me after the fight. I found it hard to concentrate on her as she had just terminated two women. Jasmin said she was satisfied with my performance but we had work to do.

We went to the car the two women had come in. Jasmin opened both doors.

"Are the keys in it?"

"Yes," I replied.

"Start the engine, my love. We are going to push it over the mountain edge. They will be lost without it. Well, it was just an accident. They went off the road and tried to get out but it was too late," she laughed out loud as it went over the mountain.

"Let's move on," I said, "In case we have been seen here."

"Good idea. But hurry. I want you. I'm hungry for you. I could eat you now."

Wow, I thought. Jasmin was playing with me all the way around the mountain. There was a private road going off the main track.

"Go up there, baby. Let's make love up there," she said.

We found an area and reversed to the edge of the road; the views of the mountains were something else.

"Let's go in the back of the van. I want you to make love to me and I want you to do it whilst I'm looking at these beautiful views."

Jasmin was like a hot potato; she was too hot to hold. She was moving around in ecstasy. She was the sexiest woman ever. I could never imagine anybody else like her. She was the best. It was as if she was on the edge of death and been given the gift of life and she was milking life to the max extracting every last drop out of it.

"Mateo, I want you again. I need to connect with you."

I thought we had been connecting for the last thirty minutes and *now* she wanted to connect. I only had to look at her and whatever she wanted, she got. We made love again. My woman was drenched from head to toe. It was as if she had just come out of the swimming pool. There was no stopping her. I felt like I had been on a rollercoaster ride where you could not get off. We were riding for England and America together.

She had won first, second and third and she wanted forth. My strength was at an end. I hadn't slept for thirty-six hours. I was totally out of it; exhausted beyond belief. Jasmin, however, seemed to have exchanged adrenaline for blood. She was full of it. I felt like an old steam locomotive trying to keep up with a high-speed train. She was belting along, not stopping for anybody and that included me. Hell's teeth.

We held each other and dropped to sleep. It was not safe but we were so tired we just nodded off. After all, we were fairly safe with Malak the Destroyer in residence; anybody coming in the van was going to be in trouble.

Chapter 30

Mateo

I woke up and it was getting dark. I wondered if the bodies of the women had been found. It was rough terrain and it could be months before anybody came across them. Jasmin had said the crows would find them first. Nobody was coming to find them.

Jasmin was still sleeping but she had been really active during the day so she deserved the sleep. Maybe it was better to drive at night as we had no papers for the van. If we were picked up by the police, it could track us back to the kidnappers. If the van was legitimate and registered to them, I was sure they would have been found by now by the builders renovating the farmhouse. We had cleared the area, and we were well on our way elsewhere.

I looked at her sleeping. Butter would not have melted in her mouth. She was lovely. My beautiful woman; her mind was at rest. Jasmin wanted to deliver a clear message to everybody to stay away from her man. After all, she was tooled up for warfare.

Jasmin woke up and it was dark.

"We will drive through the night and get to Geneva, Switzerland for the morning."

"I'm happy with that, my love," she replied and we continued the journey.

The roads were winding and dangerous at night, with not a lot of barriers to stop you going over the edge of the mountain. It was a night drive at your own peril. We could see the snow on the mountain tops. Two months later and we might not have got through the roads due to heavy snow, but we were okay for now. We had to drive at a steady pace but the views with the dawn sun coming across the mountain ranges was absolutely stunning.

We pulled into a layby to take in the views. The mist was rolling over the mountains. The sun was in a battle with the mist to win over the day. It was a splendour of sun rays above being lost in the mist. Lighting up the earth in an incredible light show not to be missed.

We could see the Swiss Alps far in the distance. The top of the Matterhorn Mountain shining in its glory with its distinct snow crooked summit fronting the Alps, like a solider guarding an ammunition store. It looked almost biblical, standing proud. If you managed the assent to the top, you might be able to reach heaven. It would be a perilous climb as so many people have died attempting the assent and failed. Many have also died on the treacherous descent. It was not for the dreamers. Only the brave had mastered its might and its presence.

"Let's stop in the first village at the bottom of the mountains," I said, "We could climb it whilst we are here."

"You first, my darling," she laughed. "If you go up, I will follow my man until the end of the earth. If he loves me."

I kissed Jasmin.

"You are my life now."

We got into Zermatt: a picturesque village nestled at the base of the Matterhorn. The mountain was like a Greek god looking over all it encompassed. It cast a shadow blocking out the sun, like an eclipse. We found a hotel for climbers; we could chill out here as it was not five-star luxury. We both looked at the mountains. What a beautiful summit. The sun reappeared casting light over the snow-capped part of heaven God had created for us.

Our plan was to hide out here for a while to hopefully let our trail go cold. We could lose ourselves here, out of the cities, and make some time for ourselves to get to know each other's strengths and weaknesses. We had a lovely room facing the Matterhorn. It could not have been better. The best view ever from the opposite side of the village. We had a balcony too. Walking out on to it, we could see all the Swiss chalet houses dotted on the mountain.

The cold air seemed to take your breath away. Breathing it in, filling your lungs with clean air, it was as if it was cleaning the grime of the cities from them. We decided to have a sleep until the evening.

We woke around 6pm. It was time to go out and eat as we would miss the opportunity here, where there were no late-night places to eat. Most people would be in training to be in perfect fitness in readiness to climb the Matterhorn. The night seemed to draw in quickly. The sky was clear; you could see every star. The twinkle from them dancing off the mountain snow brought a sparkle to the evening sky.

We had our meal and started to make our way back to the hotel. We looked around the area. It was a picture postcard. All the snow and the chalets were lit up in a warm soft lighting, glowing like the embers in a fire. It was so lovely to be with my woman, walking hand in hand. I thought about all the people that had died attributed to me as we walked. If I had not gone rogue, these people would not be dead. I knew Jasmin would have argued differently as she was all about survival of the fittest. It was their time and nothing would change it.

We got into the hotel bedroom; we had bought the last of the wine back with us. We got two glasses, filled them and sat out on the balcony looking at the mountain. We toasted to love forever and happiness. Jasmin came over to me and sat on my knee, putting her arms around me and kissing me.

"I love you more than you will ever know. I truly love you unlimited," she said. She seemed to melt in my arms.

I carried her into the room and put her on the bed. She lay there looking at me, smiled and closed her eyes. I covered her up and got in bed and went to sleep.

Chapter 31

Mateo

Jasmin was late waking up; she must have been really tired. It was mid-morning when she jumped out of bed.

"What time is it, darling?"

"It's time you were up, my darling. It's 11am."

Jasmin yawned and said, "I had a lovely sleep, my darling. I dreamt we had three children and we were all at the park feeding the ducks on the lake. You were playing football with our youngest son. I had the girls with me picking mushrooms and wildflowers in the woods. We were going to make you a nice breakfast when we got home."

"That was a really nice dream. So, we have two girls and a boy? What a nice combination. It's going to be expensive when the girls get married. That's my pension gone in a dream."

"You are mean," Jasmin replied laughing.

"Well, one day soon, my love," I said, "I would like to live here and raise a family. I could find work supporting people climbing the mountain. I could make a good living here."

"For a clever man you can be stupid sometimes, my darling. You have no experience in climbing, never mind mountain support, my love."

"You are probably right. I am in strange times at the moment. There's not that many jobs for an unemployed rogue nuclear physicist."

"Well, I'm not in a good place either. I am in trouble with my country. I could be stripped of my title, pension, my job and ultimately my life because I fell for the man I was sent to capture or kill. The man I fell in love with and still am."

"You have given up so much for me, my love. You have saved me from certain death or capture and you have kept me safe in a volatile world of espionage. A world I never knew until now."

"Sit down, my love," she said, "I need to ask you a few questions."

"Fire ahead and I will tell you what you need to know," I replied.

"The two women we have just killed. You said they spoke clear English. Do you think someone sent them to take you back to the UK?"

"I'm not sure. They seemed desperate to make sure they had me in their custody. I know nothing about them. It's not in my field to know spies or mercenaries."

"When you left England, it was your plan to sell the technology for the laser guided weapon. Is it still your intention to sell the information? If it is, I could see if my country would be willing to pay for it, that could be a way out of all of this for both of us. We could live in the US," she suggested. "Away from all of this hiding and persecution from all governments' greed. We could live in Hawaii. Have our family, the one I dreamt about. Please think about it, I beg you. I promise you won't regret it, Mateo."

"Do you think it could work? I was ready to give myself up to the British government and face the consequences of being a traitor, renegade defector or worse. Whatever prison sentence that was coming I would do it gladly if you would wait for me. We could have the family you dreamt of."

Jasmin threw her arms around me.

"I love you so much. You are my king."

"And you are my princess," I replied. "I will love you unconditionally for the rest of my life."

"You will have to leave it all to me, my darling. I need to make some phone calls to see if they will accept me back so I can negotiate our terms of surrender. We can be on our way, my love, to another world of life's luxuries:

sun, sea, sand and lots of money. I love you so much I could cry," she said hugging me.

"You have saved me. I was so worried what might have happened to us."

"I was so scared for you. We're safe now. Let me do what I do best: negotiate our way out of here. I need to go somewhere out of earshot and contact my unit to tell them we are coming in and we need safe passage home."

Jasmin had a shower and got ready to go out and phone her contacts. I wished her good luck.

Jasmin needed to use a private landline and disappeared for what was around two hours and returned saying she had been in constant talks and arbitration with third parties. She said she had been trying to negotiate the best deal for both of us. We had a deal, in principle, to allow us to make our way to a designated pick-up area for safe passage back to the USA. There was a condition. This was the deal breaker. They were demanding the microchip showing the plan for the laser weapon development tracker beam. Without it, there would be no reinstatement of rank for Jasmin or sanctuary for me. The dream of living in Hawaii would not lead to fruition and all would be lost.

Jasmin had negotiated a tax-free income for life of four hundred thousand dollars per year, shared equally between us. Payable when we landed on American soil.

"It seems like a great deal," I said. "It's not what I wanted but it's a safe haven and we need the stability of the US to raise a family and live out our life in luxury."

My woman had opened a door to love and passion replacing my quest for treachery and greed. It was the opposite spectrum to what I knew. When I started the journey in London, it was all about me. I did not have anyone so I only had my selfish self to please. Things now have changed so much that Jasmin is my only concern. Her wellbeing is paramount; nothing else matters. She is my life now and I will fight to the death to keep her. I have never dreamt about anything in my life but I wake up most days in a panic to think I could lose her.

I was ecstatic with my woman, striking such a good deal for us. She said the pick-up would be somewhere on the Atlantic Ocean, to be confirmed. Then straight on to America; non-stop to freedom. I wanted to jump for joy. It had all worked out in my favour. I had my new lifestyle, my woman and 400k a year for life, tax free. I was floating on the ceiling of the hotel room punching in the air. I was the man and, with Jasmin's help, had pulled off the deal of the century. No need to even think about making a deal with the British government. I had slide tackled them all and taken them all out.

I was talking to Jasmin about all the places we would go and visit. The world was our oyster. I was beaming from head to toe. This was my moment, my time. Jasmin seemed concerned over my excitement. She called it running before I could walk. She could see I needed to relive my frustration with the current situation I had been in and now a release strategy was on its way. Just a matter of time and it would all fall into place and we would be set for life.

"I will make some calls tomorrow to see if we can meet early and make some progress with the transfer to America," Jasmin said, "We just need the location of the pick-up place."

We went out for a walk around the mountain village. Although it was a bleak place to live, all the houses were beautiful and inviting. We felt at home here, although we were miles from any big city and we had not been bought up in a village community. We needed the excitement of being close to the city for entertainment and dining.

Although it had been snowing, the sun was out and it was really hot. We had a meal on the veranda overlooking the Matterhorn Mountain. It was a magnificent opportunity to look at the splendour of the snow-capped mountains although not the highest in Switzerland definitely the most identifiable. You were dwarfed by its prominence and statue. It was so nice we spent most of the afternoon there. We were celebrating freedom and we were drinking to it, three bottles down.

We got back to the hotel, Jasmin went for a shower and came out.

"Wow," I said, "You have caught the sun, my darling. Your arms and legs are a different colour. I love it. I think I will take advantage of the skin tone."

"Come on, big boy, let's see what you got."

That body of Jasmin's was a big invitation for someone that had drunk so much wine. Was I up for it? She had thrown down the gauntlet and I was going to pick it up and challenge her. We got into the bed and she was going for it big time. I had to make sure I could deliver the whole package. We kissed, pulling the sheets back. There my woman lay like a piece of art untouchable by human hands. I had this perfect artefact and I was being allowed to touch every part everywhere. I had been given a seal of approval to discover her innermost secrets and her body was going to tell them all. Every time I touched a sensitive place, she reacted in the format of ecstasy and surrender. My woman was giving up every secret place as my tongue caressed it, tasting for a sweet spot to concentrate on. Like a bear up a tree and its tongue in the bee nest searching for the sweetness of honey.

Jasmin had her arms outstretched gripping the headboard rails, showing the whites of her knuckles, she was holding so tight. She was levitating out of the bed as if nothing was holding her down. Gravity did not exist in this bed, it was as near to space as she was going to get. The spirit of ecstasy had entered the room and had connected with her body. She was no longer mortal but a goddess of love and beauty. Aphrodite had been reborn in Jasmin and she was loving it. No rules applied. She wanted to feel everything; her adrenaline was off the scale at boiling point.

"I want you, Mateo. I want you, Mateo," she cried out. "I'm so ready for you. Please, please now. I want you now."

We had left the door to the veranda slightly open for air. We certainly would not be able to face the guests in the hotel in the morning. The whole of the village must have heard her. We made love for over an hour. It was never going to be a first place; Jasmin wanted me to run a marathon not a hundred-yard sprint. She needed me to go the extra mile, extracting every ounce of energy I possessed. We kissed and said goodnight. My body had been possessed and it needed rest. I fell asleep and three hours later, I found Jasmin was working my private parts.

Climbing on top of me, she was hot. Her whole body was on fire. I didn't know how she did it but I was excited and she was going for it. Wow, fabulous. A passing thought was you could have too much of a good thing. I lay back and helped her burn herself out. Twenty-five minutes later and three love spots later, she was ready to sleep. She was so loving, it concerned me. How many years could I supply her needs? But that was a distant thought as we were both fully committed to love. I cast it aside and went to sleep.

I woke up in the morning, and Jasmin was spread eagled over the bed looking so sexy. Her curves were everywhere they should be, caressing my eyes as I looked at her. I could feel myself getting excited so I gently stroked her curves and where they ended. I could see her moving around as she reacted to my touch.

She half woke to say, "Darling, you are the best. I love you so much."

I stroked her breast saying, "I love you more."

She smiled and said, "Make love to me, darling."

She only had to ask once.

We made love. She had her eyes closed but she certainly knew I was there, as she fidgeted around in the bed.

"I love you so much more than you can comprehend, Mateo."

She was satisfied. There was no need for a marathon. She had crossed the finishing line and was happy and went back to sleep. She had that contented look on her face or at least I thought she did. Was I overrating myself? Had I performed to a good standard? If I hadn't, would Jasmin have bought it to my attention? Without fail!

Chapter 32

Mateo

We had a lie in and left breakfast. I was not sure I could face the hotel staff and guests. They all must have heard our love making. I felt they may all be pointing and saying, "That was them that kept us awake all night."

We walked to the start of the mountain.

"Let's see how far up we can go without rope or any aids," Jasmin said.

I had my apprehensions about free climbing but it was a bit of fun. It would sort the men out from the boys.

"Let's go for it. I'm up for the challenge," I said.

Jasmin took the lead, walking up the first part. It then turned to a slow gradient of broken rock, making it easy to climb. We could get our hands and feet into the crevices.

We continued and I could see Jasmin, as usual, going for it, climbing for the USA. Nothing was going to beat her. But I knew mountains. They were not easy and not very forgiving for fools who believed they were going to conquer them easily. There she was, up front making it look so easy. I was taking my time but she was going for gold. I shouted for her to slow down and take her time, but she continued to climb.

The mountain was beginning to lose its crevices and the mountain was getting harder to climb, having to reach for a crevice to put your hand in. I could see Jasmin reaching over, overstretching to find a crevice. This was getting dangerous but she was on a mission. I didn't know if she was doing it for me or herself. She was higher than I was prepared to go and I could see she was coming up to an overhang of rocks. It was the end. She would not be able to get around that; only expert free climbers would be able to do that. She hung there trying to decide where to go but she never thought how she was going to get back down. It was a perilous drop to her death if she let go or slipped. She had her feet on a ledge so her weight was carried but if she let go, she would fall. She could not let go. She was stuck. It was going to be harder to come down as it was a reversal of going up, where you could see the crevices as you climbed. But without a rope, coming down would be a disaster. You would have to be able to let yourself down and hold your weight whilst you tried to get your foot in a crevice. It was only for the experienced climbers.

My problem was how long could she hold on and what if the weather turned. Jasmin was in big trouble; I had to get back down and sound the alarm for help. I could wave. Somebody could have been looking through a scope at the village. Maybe they could have seen us in trouble but I said to her I was going for help. I could tell she was scared. Her legs were trembling. It would have scared the best man if he had gone beyond a safe place. I was not sure she would still be there before I got back as she could fall at any time.

I went into the first building to call the alarm.

"We will get on it," said a lady and sounded an alarm. It was a klaxon siren that sounded all over the village. Men came running to ask what was happening. I told them my lady was stuck under a ledge. They had seen it before. It was a dangerous area of the mountain.

They had emergency climbing ropes and spikes to enable them to climb. They also put on helmets with lights as they would need these to see if it got dark. I could not see her anymore; I was worried she had fallen. There was no coming back from a fall at that height.

Five men made their way to the mountain. They had a stretcher. I was concerned they would end up putting my woman on it: injured or dead. They asked about where the ascent took place and I pointed up. It was too dark to see but she had not fallen to ground level. So, we all agreed she was still up there hanging on. The wind was getting up and it looked like rain or snow was on its way. *Poor Jasmin*, I thought. If her hands got too cold, she would not be able to hold on and would fall to her death. I blamed myself for following her. Maybe if I hadn't, we would be together now. Probably in a restaurant eating a meal.

I could see the men. They were at the point where we had to look for crevices. They had not confirmed if they had seen her. They were on a short-wave radio reporting back to us. They started to tie guide ropes on their way up the mountain, to hold them if they fell. The radio was quiet as they were climbing. They were not sure if she had gone left or right as there were no crevices straight. I could not remember as we zigzagged our way up the mountain. I thought she had gone to the right as I remembered looking up as the sun was going down in the west and she was on the same side.

I said on the radio, "I'm sure she is on the right, just under the shelf."

The radio went silent again. I worried. Would they get to her before she fell?

I shouted, "Jasmin, mountain rescue are on their way. Hang on."

But I heard nothing back. She was out of range. I was panicking. My heart was on overtime, racing like a Formula One car. They had to find her; they just had to find her! My thoughts were all over the place, then I heard the radio.

"We can see her in the distance. She has gone right over. She is in a dangerous place. It's going to be hard to get her in the dark. We might have to climb above the shelf and go down on a rope to get her."

"Please hurry," I said, "She has been there over an hour now. I'm not sure how long she can hold on for. It's so cold. She did not have many clothes on when we left. She must be freezing."

"They are doing their best," the support climber told me, "If she can hold on, we will get to her."

That was not what I wanted to hear: *if* she can hold on.

"She has to hold on," I said.

The radio was really quiet. I was not allowed to speak unless they spoke to me first as this would be a dangerous practice. When you're climbing, you need your hands free and full concentration. I was still waiting as it started to snow. It was light at first, but it was starting to snow heavier and heavier. Would they even find her?

The radio came on. They had found her. She was hanging onto the rock. She said she could no longer feel her hands and she felt sick with the cold weather. She couldn't stop shivering.

The mountain rescuers told her there was a man above the overhang who was going to lower a rope and then they could lock her onto the rope and start to lower her down the rock face. The rescuer saw the rope and made his way towards Jasmin.

"Don't worry," the rescuer said, "We are here now."

He belted a harness around her and clipped her on to the rope. He shouted above, "Take the strain."

The rope tightened and he said, "You can let go now, Jasmin."

She must have been apprehensive about letting go so the rescuer clipped onto the rope and said, "We will go down together."

He slid a tie clip into the crevice. He tied on and they started the descent. It was a long way down; Jasmin did not know how far she had free climbed. I was tearful when I saw her coming down the face of the mountain. I was so glad.

"I thought I had lost you," I said, "Don't ever scare me like that again."

Chapter 33

Mateo

Jasmin reached the base of the mountain and they transferred her to the stretcher. They had done a wonderful job against all odds and saved her from certain death. Everything was against her and the only thing in her favour was the skill and bravery of the rescue team in such poor conditions. She needed to be seen by a doctor and the nearest hospital was thirty miles away. She may have had the start of hypothermia and it looked like frost had chapped the ends of her fingers. Two hours later and she may have lost some of her fingers they told her.

"No more mountain climbing for you, young lady," I said.

"No more, my love," she said, smiling. "Thank you for rescuing me and bringing help. I love you."

"I love you more," I replied.

The doctor arrived and he said all her vital signs were good. There was no need to take her to hospital but she needed rest and warmth. The rescue men took us back to the hotel and helped us upstairs to the room.

"We can never thank you enough," Jasmin said. "Thank you so much. You are my guardian angels."

Jasmin was unsteady on her feet. She was cold and needed to warm up. I took off her clothes and got her into bed. I did the same and wrapped myself around her. I could feel her heating up and driving the cold out. My woman was back. She just needed to stay warm and sleep. We would sort everything out in the morning.

Jasmin was locked around me all night. She wouldn't let me go. She was probably still holding onto the mountain in her dreams. She was warm and safe now; she had learned her lesson. I was grateful I never went up with her. We would have both perished. We could have been stuck and nobody would have known. *A good lesson learnt*, I thought.

The morning arrived and it was nearing lunch as we woke up. It had been a long night. Jasmin was really happy she was safe,

"It was a nightmare," she said, "I never thought I would get down safe, even when they came to rescue me. I am so grateful to them."

I looked at her fingers. They looked bruised but the colour was coming back so she was okay.

We exited the hotel and Jasmin said she wanted to donate to the mountain rescue fund. We found the office and Jasmin made a large deposit to the fund.

"I owe them my life and you too, Mateo. I will remember this day forever."

We relaxed for the day. We chilled out: me being me and Jasmin being herself. We needed to reflect and learn from the day before and we spent some quiet time holding each other. It was over; there was no need to bring it up again.

"Let's go and celebrate our lives and we are going to have the best champagne in the house and a lovely meal," Jasmin announced.

"Whatever you want," I said.

"It's on me," Jasmin said.

"Will your short arms reach those long pockets of yours, my love?" I joked.

"I'm sure they will, my love. I just seem to have trouble finding them sometimes," Jasmin laughed. "You are a bit too careful, my love. Let's live for the day."

We made a reservation at a local restaurant. I had decided we had to celebrate that Jasmin was alive and well. We smashed through the champagne, drinking two bottles of their best. The bubbles danced on our tongues as the champagne went down. We celebrated till the late evening. The champagne had made us forget all our troubles; a short-term fix but nevertheless a good medicine. I think we only got back to the hotel by luck, supporting each other along the way.

Jasmin collapsed on the bed; I fell next to her. The next thing I knew it was morning.

I woke up with a head like it had been hit by a sledgehammer. I needed a coffee; Jasmin was still flat out. I sat out on the balcony, whilst she was sleeping, looking at the Matterhorn Mountain. I couldn't believe we had climbed part of it, a very small part. *People that climb to the top must be so fit and skilled*, I thought. I could never see myself climbing to the top of it.

Jasmin came out onto the balcony, and she put her arms around me.

"Good morning, my love."

"Good morning? It's afternoon, my love," I said. "You're up late. Did you have a nice sleep?"

"Yes, my love. Lots of dreams again about a family and children. It seems to be on my mind, troubling me. Never mind. How are you, my love?" Jasmin asked.

"I'm good, thank you. I was thinking about America and when you might get a date. We need to catch the ship going over there so we can have our dream of a family. Strange we are thinking along the same lines. We must be made for each other."

"Yes, my sweetheart, we are. I will try and contact them today to see if they have any news for us. They are probably having to sail over direct from the USA."

"I'm ready to move out of Europe. It's not safe for us. The move can't come soon enough. I will be glad when I'm on the boat to America."

"I will get ready to go and ring them. I need a landline so I will have to find a private line to phone from. Wait here, baby. I will be back soon. Hopefully with some good news."

Jasmin arrived back around forty-five minutes later.

"Good news, my darling. They are coming for us and want us to meet in two days. The boat will be in the bay of Le Mont Saint-Michel on the Atlantic Ocean. We have to make our way there."

"We can stay here tonight and go after breakfast in the morning."

"Yes, that would be good. I've looked and it will take about twelve hours to get there, so we can be at Le Mont Saint-Michel around 9pm. I will book a hotel and meet them the following day around 2pm."

We sat at the bar around the corner, where we had coffee and pastries. They were really nice. We talked about all the things we were going to do when we got to America.

"They will probably put you through passport control fast as I have diplomatic immunity due to my status. You may be able to come with me, then we can be settled in somewhere nice. I will have to be debriefed on the operation, but after that we can be together, my love. We can look at buying a property in Hawaii and settling down and having that family I dreamt about."

"I can't wait," I replied, "I want it all to end. It's been a nightmare ever since Antibes. I haven't seen much of America except New York; I want to see lots of places there I have heard about. I want to see the White House and the Capital building. And I would like to go to Florida for a holiday. We can go to Orlando and go on all the rides in the parks and see Palm Beach. I would love to go and stay at the Breakers Hotel and play a round of golf there with you, my love."

"We might meet some famous people there," Jasmin said, "Is there any more you want to see?"

"I want to see it all. I want to see Las Vegas and see some shows and boxing matches. Can we go to the west coast? I would love to drive from San Diego to Seattle. We can call in at Los Angeles and go to Hollywood. Go down to Manhattan Beach and play volleyball and then have a jog on Carbon Beach. They call it Billionaire's Beach and we can see all the beautiful houses facing the Pacific Ocean. We may be able to see all the way to Hawaii."

"You will have to have good eyes, my love," she laughed. "It's three thousand miles away."

"Okay. But let's go soon, I want to go."

Chapter 34

Jasmin

We got in the van the next morning.

"It looks a bit worse for wear," Mateo said, "It needs a good wash. I hope the wreck gets us there."

"It's got us here so far, darling. I'm sure it will," I replied.

We made our route and started the twelve-hour drive. We talked all the way there; Mateo never left the subject of America and where he wanted to go. I had grown up there but he knew more places than me. We went from LA to Halfmoon Beach, Carmel, San Francisco, Lake Tahoe, Portland, and Seattle. He went all the way up the west coast, he was in love with the idea of living there. I told him life is always different when you're having to work there.

"Have you forgot about the income they have promised me for the microchip?"

"Where is the chip?" I asked in a sharp voice.

"It's somewhere safe, my love. I have it in the UK and I have left a copy here in Europe."

"We're supposed to bring it with us."

"No worries," Mateo said, "I can get it sent electronically. They can have it in seconds, when I ask for it to be sent."

"I don't think they are going to be happy about that," I said. "They wanted to see the chip to authenticate it is the one. To make sure the chip is legitimate and shows all the plans."

"I can sort it when we are in America and they will have it immediately."

"Okay, I will have to see if they approve what you're providing them and if it's satisfactory."

We were on time when we got into Le Mont Saint-Michel. The hotel looked over the bay out into the Atlantic Ocean. It was a beautiful view; you could see all the boats travelling across the bay on their way to somewhere else. Some were coming to offload the catch of the day for the local restaurants.

"Mateo, can we go straight out and find a local restaurant and have some fresh fish? It's late and I have an urge to eat fish tonight."

"Yes, of course. I hope there is going to be somewhere nice as I wouldn't like you to be disappointed. We know what you're like when someone disappoints you." Mateo was laughing uncontrollably.

"Very funny. Let's go and get some fish, my darling."

We could smell the food outside and followed our noses. It smelt tasty. We found the restaurant was still open, and we had the catch of the day. We had a large lemon sole and shared it between us. We looked across the bay. Tomorrow would be another day and we would be on our way to America. I wondered if they would send a warship to pick us up, probably an aircraft carrier or even a submarine. My mind was racing. We were both so close to freedom of the persecution we had been subject to. I thought we should enjoy the last night in Europe. We would soon be on our way.

We had a lovely meal followed by a dessert to die for. It was delicious. We had a look around before going back to the hotel. I wondered where the ship or submarine would stop. Could they get in the bay or would we have to meet them offshore?

We walked back to the hotel. Looking back, I could see some lights on the ocean flickering. Could this be the ship that had arrived?

Chapter 35

Mateo

When we got into the bedroom, I could see Jasmin was still upset about me not bringing the chip, but I thought it was best not to.

I woke up in the night. Jasmin's eyes were rolling, and I could see she was wrestling with somebody in her dreams. She was sweating slightly as she tossed and turned; something had been on her mind all day. The dawn light came through the gap in the curtains. I got up and opened them. Jasmin woke up.

"Close the curtains, baby. I'm tired."

"I will close them. I just want to see if our boat is in." My eyes scanned the bay. No ships in yet.

I closed the curtains and got back in bed, putting my arms around Jasmin. She acknowledged me with a loving pat on my arms and slept. I was not going to sleep. My mind was too active to sleep and all these thoughts were going around in my head like explosions of a meteor shower in space. My head was all over the place. I wanted to be able to see the ship. Why was it not here early?

Jasmin slept forever; she was making up for her restlessness during the night. Two hours went by and Jasmin was still fast asleep. I put my hand on her.

"Darling, are you awake?"

"Does it look like I'm awake?" Jasmin said in a stern voice. "What do you want with me?"

"I would like you to get up," I said in a meek mild voice.

"Leave me alone. I'm tired."

I turned away. *Shit,* I thought, *Malak is in the room.*

I could feel my hand shaking. I wasn't going back there. It was like trying to wake a grizzly bear from its hibernation. You wouldn't be getting a good welcome; it would probably eat you.

I lay there and I could feel a loose stool in my pants. I got out of bed and needed to use the toilet. I washed my pants as Jasmin woke up.

"What are you doing?" she said.

"Oh, just washing my smalls, dear. Do you need any washing doing, baby?"

There was no reply. I thought it was better to hold my tongue than lose it. I spent the next hour at the window, peeping out of the curtains for signs of the ship in the distance. *If only I had some binoculars*, I thought. *I might see it coming in. I would be able to identify it by the American flag.*

I could feel my heart beating. I was excited. I looked over at Jasmin in the bed sleeping and kept my thoughts to myself as if Jasmin could hear them. I would not have been in a good place; she was not happy about not having a good sleep. There was a nest of angry wasps in that bed. There was no way I was going near it. I could hear the angry things buzzing. I checked my coat for my EpiPen, at any moment I might have needed a shot of adrenaline.

Wow, Malak the Destroyer was in residence. Come in at your peril.

Chapter 36

Mateo

Jasmin woke up around 11am.

"Good morning, darling," she said.

Wow, talk about Jekyll and Hyde. She was worse than them. At least you stood a chance with him; she would take no prisoners. It was built into the very fabric of her. It had been tattooed into her very soul. There would be no mercy from her.

"Good morning, baby," I said, "Did you have a nice sleep?"

"Yes," Jasmin replied, "Lots of strange dreams, my love."

I thought it was best not to ask too much; her dreams could turn out deadly.

I was excited about the ship coming and kept looking out the curtains.

"Open them, baby. Let the morning into the bedroom," Jasmin said.

"I can't see any sign of the ship," I said.

"They're probably waiting outside French territory waters. We might have to be taken by a boat out into international waters to board the ship," Jasmin said. "Mateo, stop pacing around the window. We can go out soon to look. Come and have a shower with me, my love."

I took off my pyjamas and stepped into the shower with my princess. My woman looked really good. Her bruises from the fights had receded to a light brown, blending into her toned skin. As I washed her body, my hands caressed all her sensitive areas making everything stand on end. I found all the places, paying special attention to all the buttons, sending them all off at once. Jasmin had her arms in the air and hands on the shower wall tiles, scrapping her nails down the soapy walls in excessive acts of ecstasy as I found the areas only I was allowed access to. No permission was required. Jasmin had made herself available for love and I was the benefactor.

"Can we have something to eat before we go? I'm not quite sure when they eat on warships. The dining room might be open now."

"Let's keep our feet on terra firma for now until we are on it."

"I suppose you are right; I am getting ahead of myself."

We made our way down to reception and we exited the hotel into the bay. It was fairly busy with boats coming and going.

"Let's go and eat where we ate last night," I said. "We can look out for our ship. They are definitely coming today."

"Yes, they will be here soon. When they are here, they will ring me and we can go down to meet them."

"Okay. Let's go and have some food and it should be time by then. We can get our luggage and sit on the harbour wall and wait for them to come."

We had a lovely lunch; Jasmin was very attentive, holding me tight as we walked around the bay.

"I can't see any ships," I said standing on the harbour wall with my hands out pretending I had a telescope and was looking out to sea. "I see no ships."

"Get down, you silly man, before you fall over into the sea," Jasmin said, laughing. I was on a fairground ride, and I didn't want to get off. I was ready for a new adventure.

Jasmin said, "I can see a yacht coming in. This is it."

The sails were down and it was on engines rounding the bay, making its way to the harbour.

"It's a bit strange they have hired a sailing yacht to take us out to meet them," I said. "How far out are they?"

"I think they are out there waiting further than I thought."

The boat chugged into the harbour. This was a proper yacht, not something to be running on an engine, but to be running free with the wind in its sails. Two seamen were on deck sailing it. One jumped off and secured the mooring lines to the harbour walls. They continued to work on the ship as we made our way around. We got to the sailing ship and Jasmin shouted out to the men.

"Permission to come aboard."

The men put out the jetty ladder and Jasmin and I made our way up it onto the boat.

"This is a lovely yacht," I said. "Will this make it to America?"

I saw Jasmin go over to the seamen. They were talking and they made a few hand signals. I couldn't hear them talking.

"Everything is okay. We will be leaving soon. We need to get on board and get settled in."

"Get settled in? What does that mean? How long are we going to be on this yacht?" I asked in a stern voice. "When are we meeting the warship?"

"I'm not sure. They must have contracted these men to pick us up for the transfer."

"Okay," I said. "What language are they speaking? That's not French or American."

"It's broken Russian. They're just here to sail the boat."

"Well, it's not what I expected. I thought they would send a naval launch for us, not a sailing yacht. We're not going to be getting anywhere fast on this. There's no wind at the moment. I just can't understand why they would send something like this."

The men jumped onto the harbour and untied the mooring lines and pulled in the walkway. We were on our way. The engine started and they told us to sit at the front of the yacht whilst they cleared the bay. We were out the bay area when two more men appeared from the underside cabins. They didn't look like sailors; they made their way across the deck towards us.

They looked quite menacing. These were not sailors. They were here for a reason. Maybe they were marines or seals. Jasmin was looking at them in an inquisitive way. Who were these people? What were they doing?

They went over to Jasmin. They were about to talk when one took a stick out of his pocket and knocked her over the head. She was dazed. They said something in what seemed like Russian but I wasn't sure on the language. I looked at Jasmin. I could see her slouched over; her head bleeding slightly on the decking. They looked at me and grabbed my arms and took me down the stairs into the hull of the boat. They tied me to a chair and went on deck talking to the deck hands sailing the yacht. I could see them telling the sailors what to do. This, I thought, was strange. Who were these people? Why had they tied me up and what were they talking about to the sailors? I thought they were Jasmin's American friends. Why had they hit Jasmin and brought me downstairs?

My thoughts were on Jasmin. Why had they hit her that way? What had she done to deserve that kind of treatment? I could see them moving around the boat. These were not sent by the Americans. We were in trouble. These were north-eastern, not nice people, quite ruthless. Were they out to kidnap us for money?

They came down into the cabin with a toolbox and talked to me in what sounded like broken Russian. Did they have a plan? I wondered what it was.

Chapter 37

Jasmin

I started to come around. I looked up and saw Mateo had gone. I could hear screaming from below. It sounded like Mateo. I was tied up to the forward sail mast. I would have to try to escape so I could help him.

I looked over the deck. The deck hands were putting up the main sails. We were going out into the ocean. I needed something sharp to cut the ropes behind me. There was some movement of my hands. I started to wriggle them. I had been trained that when someone ties you up, you expand your body or your hands, later you deflate them afterwards. The blow to the head had not been as severe as they thought. I pretended to slouch over but I was not unconscious but playing their game.

Was there enough movement to release my hands and get free? I kept on wriggling my hands; my wrists were becoming really sore and bleeding but I had to get free. I could feel the looseness in the ropes and I started opening the knot.

I could hear Mateo making noises. I could only imagine what was happening to him.

I had one hand out of the grip of the rope. Malak the Destroyer was free. Someone was going to pay the price for their treachery. I was out for blood and was going to start killing indiscriminately. I looked at the two sailors on the boat. They would have to go first. I could see a boat hook hanging over the side of the boat. I had to get them both before they could alert the other two working on Mateo.

I went over and picked up the hook off the side of the boat. I looked and saw they were at opposite ends of the boat. One was looking over the front of the boat at the safety net. He wasn't going to be looking again as I lunged the boat hook into his neck exiting through the other side. He fell and I picked him up by his legs and threw him into the sea.

"Atlantis are looking for deck hands."

The other seaman had not seen what had happened and was at the first mast. I crept over. There was a loose rope around the pole that I picked up and lassoed around his neck. Pulling on the rope, I lifted him off the deck by his neck, hanging him. He was kicking trying to get a hold on the pole but I saw him and pulled him further up the pole. I could see he was still alive but Malak had the rope and pulled him halfway up the mast. His legs stopped kicking; his hands dropped. He was gone. I tied him off on the mast hook.

"You can rot there," I said.

Now I had to free my love. As I looked around, I could see my rucksack. I opened it. Great, my guns were still in here. I took out a sawn-off shotgun. I had gotten that at the farmhouse killing. I also grabbed a handgun and put in my jogging trousers.

I went to the entrance to the under deck and tapped on the door. One of the men torturing Mateo opened it, I let him have it in the face with the shotgun and then in the chest. He fell down the stairs. It was a gruesome death. Too quick for a bastard.

I could see him, what was left of him, smoking from the gunshot wound at the bottom of the stairs. His counterpart in crime came running up the stairs wielding a machete in his hands. I stepped back as he was coming out fast. He came out yelling and screaming, waving the machete trying to catch me and cut me up. I fell over a deck bucket moving backwards to get out of his way. He was on me, trying to hit me with the machete. I rolled over out of the way of the danger of the blade. I managed to jump up and he fell on the deck missing me.

I saw an opportunity. I jumped on his back punching him in the head. He managed to turn around and I found him on top of me. He was a strong man. I had to get him off before he overpowered me.

I reached into my jogging pants and took out the handgun. I shot him in the stomach and then between the legs. He dropped down; his head hitting the deck at the

237

side of me. He uttered a few words into my ear as I pushed him off. I stood up. He had turned, looking up at me.

"Have a bit of gunpowder," I shouted and shot him dead in the centre of his forehead. I threw him down into the hold whilst I gathered my thoughts, just missing Mateo.

I saw the whites of his eyes roll. That was the last one. I had terminated the traitors. They were all military soldiers from Eastern Europe. They had been sent to pick us up and take us back with them. I had been a double agent, living and working in America but my loyalties lay with my homeland in Eastern Europe. I had been taken from my homeland in my early life but I had a different prospective on Eastern Europe now. I saw there was going to be nothing there for me but death. How stupid could I have been to even consider going back to live in Eastern Europe. There was nothing there for me. No family or friends, just a hostile environment. I was now focused back on my real home where I was a free American.

I ran downstairs to Mateo. He was tied to a chair, and he was out of it; in a subconscious state. I could see buckets of water at the side of him and wet towels. They had been water boarding him, a horrible torture method. You put a towel over the face and mouth and pore water over the towel. It gives the impression to the tortured person of drowning as the water enters their mouth.

He was missing two fingernails on his left hand; I could see them on the floor at the side of the chair. He had been lucky, if you could have put it that way, as they had some secateurs probably to remove fingers. They had not finished their enquiries with him. It was all about timing. I managed to get to him in time before they moved on to more gruesome torture.

I released him from the chair. He thanked God and kissed me.

"You are my guardian angel," he said.

Mateo's pants were wet. I'm not sure whether it was the water boarding or the torture but he was quiet. It was probably the nearest he had been to death; these men were not put there to socialise with him. They wanted him to tell them the whereabouts of the microchip.

The boat suddenly had a scrapping noise on the underside. I ran up the stairs onto the deck. We were near some rocks and the keel was catching them.

I grabbed the wheel. As the rudder engaged, I turned it back out to open sea. With all that was going off, I had forgotten nobody was steering the yacht.

Mateo surfaced from the cabin area. He looked worse than he actually was.

"Let's clear away these bodies and clean up the boat and we can see what's on board to eat and discuss our next actions," I said to him.

I never mentioned anything about being born in Russia or being a double agent with Russia. I was never going to work with them ever again. It was just me, Mateo and

America. I had learnt a lesson I would never forget. What would they have done with me and Mateo after they had gotten what they wanted?

Chapter 38

Mateo

We sailed about five miles out towards the Channel Islands off the coast of France. We had a yacht now; the world was our oyster. We could go anywhere and it was all free. All we needed was the wind and some maps.

"Can you read the maps?" I asked her.

"Yes, my love. I have done a lot of sailing," Jasmin replied.

Wow, I thought, *is there nothing this lady hasn't done?*

Jasmin lowered the sails and said, "Let's go eat, my love."

She dropped the anchor and went to the galley. Surprisingly, it was well stocked. We were going all the way. There was going to be no transfer onto a bigger ship.

We started to clean up. The galley was dirty as the four men had made it filthy. Nobody had cleaned anything including the cups. We would have to clean up before we ate a meal.

We needed to get rid of the bodies, so Jasmin threw them overboard, one after the other.

"Give me a hand to get the two out from below deck, baby," she said.

I helped her. I could not even see a face on one of them. Jasmin did not seem bothered; she had seen it all before. After all, it was just a body now. We got to the side of the boat and dumped him overboard. We saw shark fins in the water swimming around the bodies.

"Don't worry about them. They have to eat as well," she said.

We went back to bring the last body out and threw it into the water with the others. It was getting dark and it was when most sharks were feeding, looking for food. The number around the bodies had increased. I counted twelve thrashing about, biting pieces out of them. They were in a feeding frenzy and there was lots of food for them.

Jasmin shouted, "Bon appetite."

We were going nowhere tonight. The anchor was down and the boat was going nowhere. We started the generator and the lights were on. It was a bit chilly. Jasmin moved over to me and put her arms around me. Malak the Destroyer had done her job and was gone; she was back to her loving self.

"I love you," she said.

I looked back at her and said, "I love you more."

She smiled and kissed my cheek. We could hear the sound of the sharks thrashing about, having a feast on the bodies.

"Leave them alone," she said, "They will be gone by the morning."

"You are a hard woman, Jasmin."

"Yes," she said, "If you had grown up with a stepfather like me, you would be too. I had years of abuse from him, fighting off his advances in front of my blood family. He turned me vicious and I have never forgotten how abusive he was. So, I apologise but this is the only time I will, so accept it and move on, darling."

I was silent. I had known nothing about her past. I had come from a loving family who doted on me and gave me all the love they could give.

"You had a terrible stepfather, abusive and horrible. I can't think of what you must have gone through. I'm sorry, baby. I understand why you are so uncaring. You see things in black and white where I'm on full colour all the way. I've only had happy times."

We agreed not to talk about it anymore.

"It is what it is and that's it," Jasmin said.

We were both hungry so I said I would cook. I went to see what was in the food store. We managed some rice and fish, with some chilli peppers and a French stick. They must have bought it in the harbour pastry shop. There were some nice pastries too. Someone must have liked French bakeries.

We sat outside under the moonlight on the yacht. We could see the flickering lights in the distance on land and the stars twinkling in the sky. It was a full moon lighting up the ocean. We could see virtually everything in the ocean. We could see the fish coming up for air, making circles in the water. We watched them disappear.

It was so nice to be there alive with my woman. We had the whole world in front of us. Tomorrow was another day and we would deal with it as it came. We looked back on our time together. Jasmin talked about all the good times we had. Where I talked about the people we had terminated.

"Leave them alone. Leave them where they lie," she said.

"Yes, you are right, my darling."

We spent the night on deck. We had a couple of blankets that we had found below and we wrapped them around us and fell asleep. It was late and the sun would be up in four hours.

Chapter 39

Mateo

We woke up to a noise at the side of the boat. Looking over the side, there was a pod of dolphins playing around the boat, diving under, and jumping out the water. They were so friendly. Jasmin wanted to get in the water and swim with them.

"It's a bit early, baby. Everything is eating at this time of day. You could be on the menu. I think the dolphins would protect you from anything but somebody with a gun."

"You are probably right," she laughed, "There were a lot of sharks feasting last night. I don't want to be on the menu today. I can't see any sight of the bodies we threw in last night but the sharks could be coming back for seconds."

We decided it could wait for another day. Jasmin went below to look for breakfast food.

She shouted from the kitchen, "They have a fishing rod. Can you catch us something to eat?"

"I'm afraid we will both starve if you wait for me to catch anything. I can't even catch a cold."

"Don't worry, darling," Jasmin shouted back, "I've found some bread, eggs and ham. We are in for a feast. I don't think we were going to have a share in this. We would have been lucky to live another day. They were not good men. I managed to serve them a meal they would never forget. They were the meal. At least the sharks ate well."

We sat at the bow of the yacht with our legs dangling over the sides eating a nice, cooked breakfast, looking out to sea. There was a slight breeze wafting over the ocean showing the white water, turning it into a mystical field of cotton. The whole ocean was alive and showing us in all its glory. The breakfast tasted so good I didn't know whether Jasmin was a good cook or I was really hungry. My fingers had stopped aching but were feeling really sensitive.

"Don't worry, darling. I never liked those two nails," she said, "They were your worst ones. You might grow some good ones this time."

I laughed at Jasmin, "I take it you are joking?"

"Yes, of course, my love. I hope they grow fast. You can't keep those bandages on all the time."

"Jasmin, you're in deep water. Be careful."

"You are funny, Mateo. I love you so much."

"I love you more," I said. Jasmin leant over and kissed me.

"Where are we going today, captain? We have a boat now; we need some direction, captain. Where to next? Let's weigh anchor," she said.

We decided we could not go back to the bay for the van as they would have been missed and would be looking for us. The first place would be the bay.

"I will have to be captain," Jasmin said pulling rank on me, "As I know how to sail this yacht, you will have to take the place of the deck hand and work for a change."

I looked at her in a disapproving way.

"Me? A deck hand? You have to be joking."

"Yes, of course. We will share the work. You can be a sergeant; I have to reserve rank."

I conceded.

"Okay, captain," I said and gave her the finger.

"I can have you thrown in prison and court marshalled for that."

"Carry on. Ready for duty."

"Weigh anchor," she shouted.

She started the engine as there were a few rocks that we could see poking out of the water. It would be safer till we got beyond them. As we were clearing them, we decided to go south instead of west. We would have gone into British waters at the Channel Islands and would have been met by border control who might have arrested us. North would have taken us up into the English Channel and the North Sea towards Norway. We might as well have given ourselves up earlier. South would be the only option. Jasmin had only sailed offshore and did not know how she would fair crossing large areas of ocean. Her idea was to keep sight of land by sailing offshore.

"We have everything we need, baby. We can just go on an adventure. Nobody will be looking for us out here, my love," I said.

"Hoist the main sail," Jasmin cried out.

I began to pull up and opened the sails. The wind hit the sail and the boat took off. We were on our way to a new adventure. Jasmin was in her element, steering the yacht, and we were flying along.

We had good stocks of food and we needed to make some space between the bay and us. We agreed we would sail most of the day into the evening. Jasmin asked me to take the wheel.

"Stay on this course and we should be okay," she said. "Look out for other boats or rocks. Please don't go to sleep. I'm going to find some maps so we can look for dangerous areas and strong currents that could drive us into the rocks."

Jasmin bought the maps onto the deck, and said, "It all looks good. We are clear all the way."

We set course for Brest on the peninsula around from the bay of Saint-Michel. We would make it by early evening subject to a good wind and we would need to look at supplies when we arrived. Jasmin seemed to be enjoying being the captain. She had settled down well. She had control of the yacht and was loving it. We had perfect conditions; the ocean was calm with a slight breeze filling our sails. It was enchanting.

Rounding the peninsula, we saw the pod of dolphins. They had possibly been following the yacht. They were putting on a show for us. We watched them jumping out the ocean crossing each other in a perfectly rehearsed formation dance. They kept us entertained for hours until they headed off into the wide-open space of the ocean.

We could see the port of Brest and headed for it. Jasmin asked me to take the sails down as we needed to enter port on engine power as it was more stable for entry. We dropped anchor in the estuary and took the transfer dingy into port where we picked up some fuel for the outboard engine. We picked up some food supplies and some bottles of wine. We thought it was best to spend the time on the yacht as we did not want to expose ourselves to anybody searching around for us. There was a festival of light going on in the harbour near the yacht. There was a firework display at the end of the show that lit up the sky in an amazing show of colour. It was a lovely end to a fabulous day of sailing. We had done so much today, we needed to rest. We had all we needed: somewhere to sleep, eat and chill out. We sat there on the yacht under the stars and moon. What more could we want?

Jasmin looked so good in her shorts and ripped sleeveless vest. As she moved, I could see her breasts down the side of the arm sleeves. They were perfect, totally holding their own. No need for support. As they moved, my eyes moved with them, like they were on wires connected.

Jasmin caught my eye and asked, "Do you want me? Come and feel them."

That was exactly what I wanted to do.

"Yes, darling. That would be nice."

"I will join you," she said and came over. Her vest top came off. "Come on, baby. I need you here right now."

We made love most of the night. She was vocal in her love making; most of the harbour must have heard. She was exhausted. I was destroyed completely but she was happy. I had completed, for once, what I set out to do.

"Go to sleep, my love. We can leave later in the day."

We slept out most of the night under the stars, maybe someone was looking over at us. I hope Jasmin had not woken them up in the night with our love making. Jasmin made love like she fought men: precise, and it happened all her way.

Chapter 40

Mateo

We weighed anchor and cleared the harbour inlet out to open sea. Jasmin turned off the engine.

"Raise the sails. Unfurl roller. Raise the main sail."

I was running over the yacht whilst Jasmin was at the wheel. She had turned out to be a real captain, giving orders. She was laughing as I ran around like a headless chicken. I was sure she wanted me to jump overboard.

"Tack," she shouted. She wanted to change direction through the wind to port, to head down the south Atlantic. Next stop: Lorient.

I was about to sit down when more orders came from behind that wheel they call the helm.

"Make sure you clean up the lines on the starboard deck. We are starting to heel and we don't want the mast being caught up in the lines."

I am the deck hand, I thought. *I better ask what a deck hand gets paid.*

The boat was flying out of the water. I thought Jasmin was going to turn it over but she stayed confident and just smiled as the spray cooled her face. She was in her element.

After all, she was a commander in the Navy Seals. I was sure she had captained boats before. I only had just found out my left hand from my right and now she wanted me to know my port from my starboard. She was a real taskmaster, cracking the whip. I was not used to taking orders. I was sure she thought I was under her command. Well, she would have to help out if she wanted me to make love later. My legs were like jelly now, only the lord knew what they would be like when we got to Lorient. I needed oxygen now as well. Jasmin kept calling the orders in between reading the charts. She was an expert at everything. Was there anything this woman couldn't do?

I leant over the side. I didn't know whether to be sick or throw myself over. I wanted to quit my job but the boss wouldn't hear of it. She needed a galley slave, not a deck hand. I had definitely drawn the short straw.

We arrived in Lorient. From the yacht, we could see the Keroman submarine base.

"I want to go and see that base," Jasmin said, "To look at old French submarines and compare them to ours in the same period."

"They have five ports here. It's a big sailing place. They have lots of yachts come here to race. They even have a museum dedicated to yacht racing, so we could stay a while and race."

"Don't be silly. I can only just steer this and as for you, you would collapse if you had to work hard to win. No, my love, we are not entering any race, but it looks fabulous. I would like to stay a couple of nights."

We pulled into the first harbour. It was busy; quite a vibrant port. There were nice bars with people sitting out alfresco. We had an evening dinner at the Le Crabe Marteau. The crab was fabulous; a really good service.

Jasmin was happy. She had eaten well and had one of her favourite foods: crab. We walked around the city and looked at the venues.

"We will go to these tomorrow," Jasmin said. "We will go to the zoo. I love animals, and it is a big zoo. So, are we good to go, my love?"

"Yes, of course. How could I refuse?" I replied.

We made our way back to the yacht. It looked like rain so we decided to sleep below. The beds were a bit sparce but easy to sleep in. In the morning, we decided we would find a nice bakery in the city and have some croissants, cakes and a fresh cup of coffee. We saw a big queue outside one shop, and we could see it was a bakery.

"This is the one to eat from. The size of the queue has told me," I said to her. We queued for thirty minutes and the food was second to none, the best baker for fifty kilometres we were told. We wanted to get more but the queue was twice the size so we opted to go to the zoo.

We had a great time at the zoo. Jasmin loved all the animals and reptiles. I was surprised she liked snakes and spiders. We had an ice cream as we walked out of the zoo.

A man took our picture and ran off, and I wanted to chase him.

"It's too late. He has gone. We will have to leave here as he knows about us now," Jasmin said. "There is probably somebody giving a reward for anybody that can prove where we are."

We made sure nobody followed us back to the harbour. We got on the yacht and sailed out to open sea. We were safe. But for how long? They all probably knew we were on the yacht that was missing. Their search just got bigger; they would be searching sea and land now. We would be more vulnerable out at sea if they came with guns. It would be hard for us to defend ourselves against all the would-be mercenaries of other nations. Even the French would be looking for us.

We had to abandon the yacht and travel across France to Switzerland and claim asylum in a foreign country because we were being persecuted and could be killed. We decided that we would be able to make it to La Rochelle and we could leave the yacht there and make our way across France to Switzerland.

"We have a head start as he has to get the information to his contact. They will have to investigate at Lorient to pick up a trail. Nobody saw us leave in the yacht and if they did, we could have gone north or south or over to the Channel Islands. So, we have some time unless they have use of a helicopter or plane to spot us. Let's get all the sails out and make this baby fly."

The boat was heeling. I was hanging on a line so I didn't fly off. Jasmin was taking the boat out to the max; the keel was virtually out the water, but we were making good time. It would not be long before we reached La Rochelle. All the sails were up and we were flying.

Chapter 41

Mateo

I could see the coast of La Baule as we passed it. It would not be long now. Jasmin was in her element. She was not bothered about anything. She was loving steering the boat; being master of all she commanded.

"Track," she shouted. She was about to change direction through the wind. I hung on as Jasmin was belting along and the turn could be dangerous, especially with Jasmin at the helm. We were back on course. I had a slightly nervous stomach as she was quite aggressive with the wheel. She thought she was in the Vendee Globe boat race to La Rochelle. The ocean was turning a bit rough. We were getting large swells coming on. We needed to get to port in case there was a storm coming.

It was evening and the dusk sun was starting to disappear below the horizon. Soon, we would only have the moonlight to navigate by. Although the ocean was getting rougher, there was a calmness about the ocean. It was as if it was holding the storm back until we were safe on dry land.

"La Rochelle on the port side," Jasmin shouted.

I crossed the boat to look at the coastal view of La Rochelle.

"Furl the sails and lower the main sail," Jasmin said. There she was giving orders again.

We had to go in on engine as there was an old castle style entrance to the old port.

"Lines to the port side," she said, as she steered towards the harbour walls. It was fairly quiet, so lots of room to moor the yacht. We tied up the yacht and put our bags together. Jasmin left the keys in the steering column.

"It's all yours," she said as she got off and walked around the harbour into the city. We had to have a hotel, preferably not in the centre, where we could eat as we had not eaten since leaving Lorient. We needed food and a bed for the night. I thought I would treat my woman after turning that wheel all day out at sea. I managed a four-star hotel, seven hundred metres from the centre. We had a nice walk there. My land legs had returned to some normality and my stomach stayed where it should be, in place of it rolling all over the yacht. I had left the fish happy. I had fed them all day.

Jasmin put her arm into mine and squeezed it.

"You might make a good sailor one day, my love. I would like a yacht like that for us one day," she said.

I laughed and said, "Not."

"Does that mean no, baby?"

"That's right, my love."

"You are no fun sometimes, Mateo," she laughed.

We got to the hotel. It had been a kilometre walk and we were ready for a good meal and a bath. My bones were aching.

"I'm up for that bath," Jasmin said. Wow, she was hot again.

The blood drained from my face. I was sure I looked like a vampire needing a litre of blood. My face had turned to a luminous glow, and I never commented.

"You look ever so pale," she added.

A hot bath and bed that was all I needed. She hadn't been running a marathon on the boat, exhausting my energy and now she wanted to drain me more. Could my heart take the strain? I had struggled to climb the stairs to the room. We had a wash and got ready to go out for dinner. We found a steak house. I needed the protein as Jasmin was going up-scale. She was touching me inappropriately, so I knew I would have to provide special services for the commander later.

We ordered steaks as we were both really hungry. It felt like we had not eaten for a week. Jasmin was playing footsie with me under the table. She had taken her shoes off and was rubbing her feet up my legs. My hair stood on end as she took her foot higher till it was in my lap. There was a table leg in front so how the hell had she managed to end up in my lap? And I needed the toilet.

"There's no way I can get up now, is there? You are disturbing me. It will be ten minutes before I can go to the toilet."

"Give them all a show," she said, laughing.

"That's all right for you, my love. What are you going to do when there is a queue of ladies asking for my number?"

"There would be no queue if I found anybody after my man," she said in a sharp tone.

The steaks arrived; they were massive. We were so hungry we ate it all.

The waiter said, "Would you like to see the dessert menu?"

We both said no thank you in a synchronised sentence. We were so full. We sat for an hour and downed two bottles of wine. Jasmin had more than her fair share, so she was tipsy. My services would not be needed tonight.

I woke up to Jasmin wrapped around me. She was touching me. She was awake and wanted to make love. Me, not being a morning person, tried to sleep. But she was persistent in her pursuit of happiness and she knew what made her happy. Who was I to deny her happiness? She was a beautiful woman who needed my attention. We made love; the whole hotel must have known as she was very vocal.

We got ready and went down for a late breakfast. I was sure the whole hotel was looking at us. But I think it was Jasmin's beauty that attracted attention. Strange. If they had known the other side of her, they would not have dared to look. She was Malak the Destroyer and she had earned the name.

We got back to the room, and Jasmin still had not finished with me and wanted me again.

"I want it in the shower. Me and you and a lot of soap and steam."

She undressed. I could see it was an offer not to be refused. Looking at her, I felt how lucky I was to have such a beautiful sexy woman. She was love on tap and it was flowing continuously. We could not see for steam, but we were feeling not looking and enjoying every minute of the moment of ecstasy.

We had to make tracks so we exited the shower and got ready to move. We needed transport.

Jasmin said, "I will get us some."

"No," I replied, "Let's get the bus."

We walked to the bus station. Jasmin was complaining about having to walk and catch a bus when we could have had a car.

"Yes, my love," I said, "But the police would not be too far behind us. We do not want people reporting the car as stolen, bringing more attention to ourselves. They would report it the moment they knew it was missing and we would be arrested for stealing the car and they would lock us up. Then everyone would know where we are and they would be bidding for us."

We needed to go east back to Switzerland. It might be a safer place to go. We were like nomads wandering around with no home to go to. We would have to ensure we were safe.

We caught the bus to Saintes. We were on our way. I was tired, so I got my head down. We had a long way to go to reach our destination. At least we were safe and nobody was following us. We would change at Saintes to Leon. It would be around an eighty-minute ride and then onto Leon.

We arrived at Saintes and transferred buses to Leon. Jasmin was not happy.

"I'm sure we could have gotten here faster in a car and in more comfort. There's no air conditioning in here. It's like an oven. I feel like a chicken roasting," Jasmin complained.

I leant over and said, "You're my chicken, my love."

"You will be in that pissing oven if you don't sort it out," she replied.

I thought it was best to keep my mouth shut. She looked dangerous when she was angry. Best not wake the sleeping giant. Malak was inside her somewhere, looking to break out. God help who was in the way when she did. I decided sleep would be the safest way to avoid her. Six hours to go and we would be in Leon. I felt Jasmin's head rest on my shoulder. She was going to sleep too. I was happy she was calm and had accepted it was what it was. I was safe for the time being.

The bus stopped. Jasmin looked up fast. There was somebody exiting the bus, no new passengers. She slept with one eye open. She relaxed and went back to sleep. We were safe at least till Leon. It was a large city. Maybe we could lose ourselves in a big city.

We would have to transfer tomorrow as by the time we arrived the connection to Switzerland would have left, so we needed to stay overnight. I looked on the internet. There were plenty of vacancies. I thought we could do a walk-in and negotiate a good room rate.

At last, we had arrived in Leon. We came across the large river and crossed it into the bus terminal. It all seemed quiet. That was good. We just needed a hotel and something to eat. I thought we might have room service tonight with a nice bottle of wine and have an early night as the bus for Geneva was leaving in the morning at 7.50am.

Jasmin woke up. She looked refreshed.

"I love you, Mateo," she said.

"I love you more, my love. I'm glad you had some sleep, my darling."

I felt I could breathe again; she was the best woman any man could wish for when she was happy but if you got on the wrong side of her when she was mad, you might lose some valuable parts of your body. She was a volcano sleeping and it was best you tip toed passed it.

"Well, we are here, my love. We have gone full circle. Look, we are back in Leon. We have come a long way."

Jasmin yawned and said, "I'm hungry and sweaty. I need to have a shower, darling. Have you booked anywhere?"

"No," I said, "I thought we could get somewhere close as we have to be on the bus at 7.50am."

"Okay, baby. Let's look for somewhere fast. I need a hotel."

We walked around and found a metropolitan style hotel.

"This will do," she said.

We booked in and went to the room; it was not our usual style but it was perfect for one night. Jasmin dumped her bag.

"Let's go out to eat," she said.

The area was a bit dead; nothing was happening. We needed to walk a bit further to find some restaurants and bars, and we found an Italian restaurant. It was a family-owned place. There was a nice atmosphere inside with the staff singing and dancing around the tables.

"This is my culture," I said. All the food, the pasta and pastries, were all made in house. I explained how they made it to Jasmin, but she wasn't really interested. She was starving.

"Can we have some bread and olives?" she asked.

The waiter said, "Yes, madam, straight away, belle. Do you want to see the wine list?"

"Do you have a nice bottle of Tuscany Chianti?"

"Yes, madam," the waiter said. "I will bring you one out."

Jasmin tasted the wine and asked me to taste it.

"It has the sun of Tuscany and the smell of the lavender fields in it. Please pore it," I said to the waiter. "It reminds me of home. Thank you, darling. It was a good choice."

We had good food and became very friendly with the staff. They were very good and welcoming. I was right up there with my newfound family; they were all from Tuscany. That made it even better.

We stayed till the early hours of the morning and then made our way back to the hotel. As we were in sight of the hotel, there was an incident between two men and a couple. The men were asking the man and woman for something and shouting and pushing the man. The lady was clearly upset by this.

"We have to help them, Mateo," Jasmin said and we walked over towards the men. The men became abusive and started to punch the man.

The lady was crying out, "Leave him alone."

They were American or Canadian. Jasmin started to run to the man attacking the Americans. She grabbed his arm twisting it as she hit the side of his head with the palm of her hand. She shoved his arm up his back that far and kicked his legs. He went down and she pushed his arm up quick. You could hear it snap. The other attacker stood there in disbelief. Jasmin pushed him onto the floor. You could see his arm was everywhere and would not stay in any position; it was hanging behind him. She looked at the other man. He put his arms in the air. He didn't want trouble with her. I stood behind him in a threating pose.

Jasmin went up to him.

"Do you want some?" she said.

"No, madam," he replied.

She put her hand up to hit him and he stepped back so she lowered her hand. She pointed to his friend kneeling on the road.

"Take him with you."

As he helped his friend, Jasmin said, "He won't be causing trouble any time soon."

She had done a good job on him. The man and lady thanked us both for coming to their aid. Jasmin asked what had brought them to Leon. They said they were on work business but not connected. The men had followed them back from a conference meeting. They thought they would be safe walking back to the hotel. They were at the same hotel so we walked back with them. They were asking Jasmin lots of questions about the way she fought the man. Jasmin never gave away who she was. The two men had met Malak the Destroyer for a brief encounter; one they would never believe happened or forget.

Chapter 42

Mateo

We walked into the reception area. The man and woman thanked us again for helping them out. We said our goodbyes and went up to the room.

Jasmin, as normal, was hot for love. She had invoked Malak again and I think her lust for blood and battle turned her on more. We got into bed, and she was straight on me. She was absolutely beautiful. For saying she was a killer, there were no calluses on her hands. They were real lady's hands. Not sure how she kept herself so attractive yet deadly. She kissed me so softly and gently, I struggled to understand how she could fight hand to hand yet not have parts of her body hardened for battle. Every part of her represented a top model you would expect to see on a catwalk in New York or Paris, not a battle in Leon.

She put her arms around me and said she wanted me to hold her tight. She wanted to belong. She had too much of being single. Available to men that did not deserve her. She said she had never loved a man so much. I was proud in what she said, looking down at her perfect body. Her bottom seemed to be a work of art that an artist had spent years on getting the curves right and in exactly the right place.

I ran my hand over her curves. Jasmin reacted to every movement I made. She was really horny but trying to get the best out of my hands before committing to an unparallel love session. She rolled over onto her back, looking at her everything touched all the right buttons. No matter how many times we made love, it was always better than the time before. She lay there whilst I was discovering her. I wanted to turn on the light. She was so beautiful I wanted to see every bit of her and not hide her away. She spread herself over the bed. It was my time to do what I did best: give my woman all the love she deserved. I knew that only love was coming out of Jasmin for me, although sometimes I questioned it. I was sure it was true love unlimited. She held nothing back and put everything into it. What an experience to have such beauty lying in a bed next to me, surrendering her love to me. She was unparalleled in her love and she showed me every time we made love. This was love, never sex.

Jasmin was tearful after making love. She said it was because she loved me too much. Jasmin was a gift to me from the gods and so was I for her. God had matched us well and bought us together. Our names had the same meaning and it was fate that we met. We needed to sleep. We would be up early and on the way to Geneva. Jasmin seemed to go to sleep straight away. I was looking at how beautiful she was as she slept. I lay there. She was so peaceful, but my thoughts took me back to what a warrior she was.

Soon it was morning and we needed to shower and go. No time to have breakfast. We would have to hope we stopped somewhere en route to get something to eat.

A couple of hours into the nine-hour coach trip, we called at a service area for a toilet break. Lucky for us, they had a bakery in the cafeteria. We had a baguette and a coffee and returned to the bus for the rest of the journey.

We pulled into Geneva bus terminal around six and a half hours later at about 4.30pm. Jasmin had slept most of the way, she was tired after a busy night.

We got off the bus and Jasmin said, "Where to, darling?"

I thought we should probably find some accommodation but we had arrived mid-afternoon.

"Let's go and sit down somewhere, my love, and have a coffee."

Jasmin replied, "Good plan. I could do with a nice cappuccino. We can sit outside somewhere as the weather is nice."

We walked along the high street and we could see a Swiss style chalet café with a wooden veranda slightly out of place amongst the modern buildings. We had views looking towards the lake. We sat down and ordered two cappuccinos and two pastries. It was so nice here. The air was not dirty like other cities; it was clean. You could taste the freshness in the air. Your lungs seemed to exit your body like they were craving oxygen. A slight breeze drifted fresh mountain air over from the lake. It made your lungs desire and possess every bit of it.

We stayed for another coffee then found a hotel, just off the main street.

"This'll be fine for now," Jasmin said. "I'm happy here."

"Ha, that's a first," I said. "Let's go up to the room for an hour and chill out."

We got to the room. It was a bit sparce; not the luxury we were used to. But it was clean and warm.

Jasmin showed me how warm it was. She had removed all her clothes, including her underwear, and lay on the bed. She was a head-turner. I looked at her lying there on her front; her hair draped over her back nearly touching her curvy bottom. Her legs as smooth as silk, fidgeting around trying to find an area of the bed to accommodate her curves. Her head turned, looking at me, smiling. The whites of her perfect teeth seemed to glimmer like fresh snow.

"Come on, Mateo. I want to feel you, my darling. I want to be close to you. You know how much I love you. I want you to love me as much as I love you."

I lay on the bed and kissed her and whispered, "I love you more. You are my life now. I could never see me without you. I will love you till the end of time, even in death. We will be together. It is God's will."

We lay there together in a loving embrace; it was so tranquil and as she moved, she excited me. She rolled on top of me. She was a goddess of love and she was going to show me how she earned the name.

I could not believe the positions she could manipulate herself into. She wanted to make love in so many ways. She was a gymnast, ballerina and contortionist all rolled into one special woman. This was Jasmin at her best. There was no runner up in sight. She had won every race. I was so happy she was mine and she had shown that for the last sixty minutes.

We drifted off to sleep and woke up around 5pm. I was hungry. We had not eaten much and we had been up so early. We decided to go and see what was happening in Geneva. We wanted to eat as we walked, so we found a takeaway. We saw a pavement takeaway cabin, selling German sausage cobs with fried onions. Just the smell tempted us. We shared one; they were far too big to eat one yourself. We shared it as we walked arm in arm. Jasmin reaching up when she was ready for another bite. It was gone in less than five minutes but we enjoyed the experience of sharing our food.

Maybe we should do this more often. It was nice to be able to share in place of always eating alone. Me with mine, her with hers; it was a better experience to share. It bought us more together as one. That hot dog had done more than just feed us; it had changed the way we would do things in the future. We would order sharing food and share the love of food as a close equal to sharing ourselves in love. After all, food was the way to the heart and we would need to practise it more.

It was starting to snow as we walked around all the shops. Lights were coming on like a display of glow worms in a mountain side showing the way. This was a place where billionaires lived and I could see why the crime rate was so low here. Most of the population was rich and there was no need for crime, bar the odd pickpocket, usually a foreign national coming in for the purpose of relieving the pockets of others for their own greed.

If you were rich and looking to retire, there were only two choices for me: here or Monaco. You could live out the rest of your life in a lavish and safe environment. We had been walking for two hours; Jasmin checking out the shops, me checking out the prices. We were a team. She perused and I held the purse. Obviously well zipped up. We had to make the money last. I didn't want her to exhaust all her account that had probably taken a long time to accumulate. We were looking for a pay day but it was not coming too soon.

We moved around the continent looking for refuge, a safe haven where we could live in peace. I was sure we were just fooling ourselves; we needed some clarity on where we were going with all this and where it was going to end. We were going to have to take it one step at a time, and find somebody we could trust to deliver a solution to our problems.

Chapter 43

Jasmin

I had told a lot of untruths. I had created an American "golden fleece" to trick Mateo into boarding a yacht to northeast Europe. Without knowing he had been served a poison chalice, I had fabricated the whole story of the American dream. There was no four hundred thousand dollars tax free for life money or any other dream. I had been given a mission to capture or kill him. My government would be as ruthless as any other to obtain or steal the laser weapon designs. It was a weapon breakthrough that everybody would kill to have first. I wondered what would have happened to Mateo if I had turned him over. Would they have been any different? After all, they had not sent me with a big payoff for him. Just me and my guns to kill him if I could not take him. I pondered with my thoughts. Who out there would look after Mateo? Even his own government had sent out their own spies to kill him.

We were between a rock and a hard place. We had to find a compromise to all this and not let it consume us in treachery and deceit. Surely somebody must have a way out for us but it seemed every nation wanted to steal the chip; nobody was offering anything but death. We needed to either sell it and disappear, or put it on the internet as common knowledge and he who dared would win. There could be no winner in this as it could only cause a nuclear war between all nations. We were in a dilemma as to what to do. We needed to at least get to a neutral country so we could negotiate a deal or surrender in peace. We could not keep fighting them.

We got up early as we needed to move fast. We did not know who the men that attacked the couple in Leon were. Had they mistaken them for us? After all, they were near our hotel and staying there.

The more I thought about it, the more I thought it was true. They were out looking for us. It was too much of a random attack. I told Mateo. We hurried as we needed to get out of the city of Geneva. There would always be mercenaries wherever we went but governments would be less likely to send military personal into foreign countries who were allies.

We got on the bus and we were off. I held onto Mateo like he was made of platinum as we sped along on the bus.

"My love, you have left a lot of carnage behind us for the Europeans to clean up."

"Don't worry, my love," I replied. "We have kept them busy clearing up rubbish."

I smiled as he looked in horror. I wasn't a bit bothered. I was Malak the Destroyer.

Chapter 44

Mateo

How would this all end, I asked myself, looking at my stunning woman at the side of me. The killer extraordinaire. It made me realise you didn't really know anybody in life. You could look at a random person, man or woman, and know nothing about them. What they did or what they were about. *A frightening outlook,* I thought. You never knew anything. Yet looking at Jasmin made my heart melt. She was also my angel, my love.

We had caught a bus and now we needed to change. I woke up Jasmin to get ready to exit the bus.

She smiled. Her infectious smile commanded all my senses to be on attention. She was as beautiful as a coral snake that makes you want to pick it up and be friends. The coral snake, although the second most venomous snake in the world behind the black mamba, had caused only one death in the last seventy years. Jasmin was up there with the black mamba. She had caused so many deaths, she had the same results as a bite from the black mamba: certain death. As I looked into her eyes, they were captivating. I was being hypnotised by a king cobra; stunningly beautiful but deadly as hell.

We got up out of our seats walking down the aisle. I looked at her walking. She was perfect in every way. She walked like she was on a fashion catwalk, showing off a new collection of clothes. She made everything she wore look good. Her figure and looks complemented them all. We managed to catch the connecting bus to Montreux. It had been snowing and the snow ploughs were out clearing the roads looking over the mountains. It looked like a Christmas postcard, as we rounded the lake. The sky was dark at the mountain top. It looked like it was going to be a white-out. This was when the snow came down so thick and fast you would not even be able to see your hand in front of your face. The lake looked like a millpond; not a ripple in sight but it looked cold and uninviting. There would be no skinny dipping in there today.

You could tell the season was moving on. Some of the cars had been abandoned along the side of the road. The snow had come earlier than normal and it had caught the locals out. They were struggling to keep the roads open. The bus was sliding around; the tyres trying to find some clear area of road to grip on. We were still moving and getting close to Montreux. We could see the promenade facing Lake Geneva. It was beautiful. The houses and hotels facing out to the enormous lake stretching all the way back to Geneva. The Swiss Alps in all their glory looked over us in their might protecting us from the winds and snowstorms. The bleakness of the mountains maintained their dominance over the lake looking out as far as you could see, as the horizon disappeared with the sky melting into the curvature of the earth. We felt like we were in God's hands and this might be favourable to see no harm came to us. We could only pray as it was his call.

We had a hotel on the promenade overlooking the lake, possibly some of the best views ever. We could see the reflections of the mountains in the lake, bouncing back like a mirror. The snow-covered mountain caps glittered in the water. This was heavenly from our balcony. Although deep in snow, people were walking about on the promenade as if it was a summer's day. It seemed the cold and snow did not affect the locals. It was what they were used to and geared up for. There was a sense of solitude and peace as we watched the local residents go about their daily routine. We felt at ease, and hugged each other. This could have been the place we could have fallen in love. The magic was in the air as it drifted over from the mountains. There was a feeling of calm all around. Maybe this could be a place to lay foundations and start a family. You could smell the wealth in the area. People were rich that lived here and nothing was going to spoil their paradise.

The price of living here would be really high.

Chapter 45

Jasmin

"Yes, it looks really expensive," Mateo told me.

"But everybody is so friendly. We fit in here, darling. I really do love the place," I replied.

"More than me?"

"Never more than you, my love. You are the best. We will fit in here just fine. We will have money to live anywhere we choose."

I had not told Mateo I didn't have a plan. I didn't know how to tell him there was no money. We would be lucky if we ever found work again. We would both probably be without a country to live in. We only had limited money left. How were we going to live or eat when the money had gone? We had to possibly try to get Mateo back to the UK. They were more likely to accept us without refusal. There would be a price to pay but there was no real alternative but they would see we were looked after at least until their decision was made.

If Mateo gave back the information he had stolen, it could go in our favour and the British would still have their secrets. The weapon technology would be safe. All we had to do was get to the UK. It would be a perilous journey as once the global governments found out we were turning ourselves in, they would come at us with everything they had to get the microchip. I just had to convince Mateo. What would he say when he found out? I had exaggerated the truth to the biggest lie ever. How could he ever trust me again? Let's not rock the boat too soon, as the last thing we needed was to be obstructive with each other. I needed to keep Mateo in the dark like a mushroom until the time was right to come clean and tell him the truth. I was not sure he could handle it. I thought it best not to say anything. He could go on overload and spark out. My thoughts were: let's keep costs low and try to get to the UK as fast as possible. We might be able to negotiate from a position of strength.

We walked along the promenade but it was getting difficult to walk in the snow. Mateo was lagging and having to be dragged by me. He said I was marching and to slow down as he was tired.

"Shall we go and have something to eat? I'm hungry. Let's find a local place behind the promenade," I suggested.

Chapter 46

Mateo

We walked across the road and down an alley between the buildings. Jasmin looked down the road.

"That's the photographer that took our picture. Stay here. Don't let him see that you have noticed him."

She ran like Usain Bolt into the next street and as I sneaked a look, I saw her like a ninja come round the back of him. She chopped his neck with her hand, and he went straight to the floor. She knelt down, hand chopping at his throat in some kind of frenzied attack. After the mutilation had finished, she held up his head and gave it a sharp twist. I ran over.

"What are you doing?" I asked her. "You have killed him in cold blood."

"Well, the asshole won't be taking anymore photos with that broken neck."

Jasmin was brutal. There was no mercy. She grabbed him by the shoulders and pulled him behind a waste bin.

"Leave him there. The police will pick the vagrant up and take him in for loitering." She held my hand and said, "Let's hightail it out of here before the calvary comes. That will put the crime rate up. The place isn't worth living in."

I looked in disgust. My eyes were looking forwards. I didn't look at her. I had Malak on my arm, the psychotic murderess. She was laughing.

"Well, he took his chances," she said, "He will be on his way soon. I can feel him leaving. Let's eat, I'm always hungry after I've been to the butchers."

We saw an Italian restaurant.

"Let's eat here, Mateo. It reminds me of Tuscany. It was so beautiful there. I loved every bit of our time there."

We managed to get a table and ordered. It was all homemade and cooked on the premises. The smell of bread was fabulous. Jasmin was really hungry and she wanted some fresh bread and olives. My stomach was not feeling too well, but I hoped the food was good. I didn't want them to upset her.

She was hypersonic floating somewhere between hell and a dark place. Maybe this was heaven to her. I had a different view on heaven. I thought it best not to discuss it or I might get to see it now. She was nothing short of terrifying but I must be as sick as her as I loved her more than my own life. Everything was on the line for her. There was no turning back. They were all just casualties of war, she implied. Who was going to miss them turds?

We both had spaghetti bolognaise homemade; one of the best we had tasted. Thank the lord I thought at least the meal passed off okay. I got my cap and coat, and Jasmin's jacket and we walked back towards the promenade.

As we turned the corner, we looked down the side street where we could see the coroner putting the body of the photographer into the van.

Jasmin said, "Mateo, take your hat off. Respect the dead."

Wow, if I did that every time she killed somebody, the hat would be a worn-out old rag. We continued back to the hotel; Jasmin was humming a tune as if nothing had happened. I was sure she had a screw loose somewhere. I definitely thought she wasn't a full shilling. I must have been as mad as her.

We got to the hotel, and she was still humming the tune. We got to the room, and the humming stopped. She was hot. She wanted to make love. She was trying to pull my trousers down as she undressed herself. I was her man and I would have to do my duty, come rain or shine. She wanted me to show her some good loving.

I found it difficult to concentrate on her as she wriggled in the bed. She wanted me, all of me. She wanted me and her to be connected, no holds barred. She was wild. Everything was going to be acceptable. All of our innermost fantasies would be played out today. Our bedroom would be a fairground ride. All hands were off the barriers with all dares taken. She was explosive in her love making and was excited like never before. Jasmin was a rocket on a launch pad fired up ready to blast off. I wasn't sure if I was up to it but I was one of the main participants in this cinematic action thriller. It was a new experience for myself. I had never ever been with a woman with such an insatiable appetite for love and passion.

She screamed, "I love you, Mateo."

"I love you more," I whispered.

I could see Aphrodite was lying there. The goddess of love.

She looked absolutely stunning. How could I not love somebody that had everything every woman would die to have? She had the face and figure of a goddess. She was as hot as molten metal. All the love flowing out of her in moments of ecstasy. She made everybody I had ever been in love with in the past look like a none starter, falling before the first hurdle. She was a thoroughbred going for the gold cup. Nobody came close. She was miles ahead of everyone. No one stood a chance; there was no competition. My woman was a born leader, a perfectionist in every way. She gave everything to the man she loved and held nothing back. She was my angel. We made love all night. I was not quite sure how but it was the best workout I had ever had. I had adrenaline running wild through my veins. We eventually slept and woke late morning.

Chapter 47

Mateo

Jasmin was lying in bed thinking. She said we needed to move out of the area. It would be dangerous to stay. The police would be out investigating the murder. We didn't want to be held as suspects as we were new in town and would be detained. We had to make tracks back to the UK.

"Why back to the UK?" I asked.

"I think it's going to be safer there than here. And we might be able to claim asylum there if you give all the microchips back. It would make our sentences less and we could be together again in a couple of years," Jasmin said.

Her idea was a total turn around to what we were planning. What about America? Why was she now wanting to go back to the UK and claim asylum? Why would she not go back to the USA and take up the offer she had been promised?

I was amazed she would have even said something like this: us going to jail. What about our dream of going to

America, touring, and living in Hawaii, having a family? Where was all this going? Why would she accept going to jail and claiming asylum? Why would she not want to go back to America?

I had to ask her. We had to thrash the plan out between us to find the reason why she did not want the dream anymore. Had she fallen out of love with me? Was I the reason? I wrestled with my thoughts. We had been so close last night, so in love. Yet today… It was as if our world had been turned upside down. I wanted clarity on where we were as a couple. Did love still exist between us or was it just sex now?

My heart sank to think it could be the latter. I had to make the right decision before writing off the beautiful relationship we had. How would I ever replace her? I could never love another like I loved her. We had to find a way out of this.

"We will have to move out of this area today, my love. We can't stay here. The police will be making their enquiries and we have no alibi as to where we were and we could have been noticed in the area. Let's have breakfast in the hotel and make a move to Dijon in France, out of Switzerland. We can decide what the next step will be from there. It is two and half hours by train. We can catch the 11.30am from the train station here, my darling. We will have a nice journey through the mountains. The views will be breath-taking. I think I will be okay on the train, although I would prefer it if you would let me steal a car and make our own way there."

"We're not having any more deaths. You have killed half the population already. No stealing cars. Let's get the train. It's safer for everybody."

We made our way down for breakfast. It was continental: no bacon and eggs today, just cold meats, cheese, and bread.

"This is mouse food. Not fit to eat. The coffee is instant," I said, "I'm not even going to go there. What kind of place is this? I told you to read the reviews. Look at what we've got to eat. The mice are starving here, even they don't want it."

"Eat up, my love, you need to line your stomach or you will not travel well on an empty one."

I picked at little bits, picking up the meat.

"This is all dry around the edges and the bread is old. It's got mould on the end of it."

We decided not to eat in and we went out. We found a nice bakery, sat down and had a panini with bacon and egg. A big smile came over my face. I was happy now, enjoying the breakfast. The coffee was freshly ground so we had hit the bell here.

We made our way back to the hotel afterwards. We could see a lot more people milling around. They did not seem to be doing much. We noticed they were not actually going anywhere, just hanging around shops. We weren't sure if they were waiting for them to open but they seemed ill-matched. They were together. Some men and women but not embracing each other or holding hands. They were all smoking. It was a bit of an eastern European habit. It was strange. They were all smoking but keeping away from each other.

"We could be in trouble here, darling. Something is not right. The hair on my arms is standing up. I'm really concerned. There are too many of them if they are together. Let's walk along the promenade instead of going back to the hotel. They might come in if we are there alone. At least there are some locals walking dogs. They won't try anything whilst there are people around," Jasmin said.

We walked down by the lake. We could see the shops opening but nobody was going in. We knew we were going to have some trouble coming and we needed to have a plan or we could be in a dangerous place with nowhere to go. If we went to the police, they would probably hold us for the murder of the photographer. Jasmin had put us in a tight spot. We could not run or stay. We would be in more danger if we stayed as there would be more every day until the jackals were all fighting for scraps. Us being the scraps.

We had to get on that train alone without them getting on but how could we do it without them getting on? Jasmin had a plan.

"The bakery we were in had external toilets at the rear of the building. I could slip out the back and go get the train tickets. The station is fairly secure. If we can get there two minutes before the train goes, we can rush through the barrier and get on the train before they can purchase tickets. They won't be able to follow in time and they won't know if we are going north, south, east or west."

"It sounds like a good plan. Let's do it. I will stay visual in the bakery so they can see me. They will think you're still there. Be careful, my love, that they are not outside the hotel."

"Don't worry, darling. I will be okay. You just need to come out and walk to the station at dead on 11.30am. I will make sure I have the tickets ready. We can hang about outside till they announce the train is coming into the station. We can wait for the queue to go down and join it. Then it will give them less time to get on the train."

"Okay," I said, "I'm on it. Let's go to the bakery. I will see you later."

"Let's not kiss," Jasmin said, "It might be construed as goodbye and they will be on to us."

We made our way back into the bakery. We were rubbing our hands and our legs to show we were cold and going into the bakery to get out of the cold weather. They would just stay outside smoking; it seemed the eastern Europeans liked to smoke more than eat. As we looked outside, they were all in the same place, like soldiers on patrol outside a palace walking the same steps.

"Okay, my love," Jasmin said. "I'm going for it. Wish me luck."

"Good luck, darling," Mateo said, "Stay safe, my love."

Jasmin got up and went to the rear of the shop and went outside to the toilet area. She would be gone in a second back to the hotel.

Chapter 48

Jasmin

I rounded the corner to the hotel. There, I saw two of them: a man and a woman on the corner of the street next to the hotel entrance. I had to distract them somehow. I saw some bins belonging to the hotel and pulled them over and kicked one round near the corner into the street and hid behind the other bins at the back of the hotel. The man came around the corner to see what was happening. I had an empty bottle of prosecco out of the bin in my hand and leapt out, smashing it over his head. He fell to the ground; he was out cold.

I went to the corner. The woman must have heard the glass smashing and was on her way up to investigate. She came around the corner but I was ready for her.

I turned her, grabbing her around the neck and dragging her around the corner out of the side street. She was struggling to breath. She had Malak the Destroyer's arms around her neck, strangling her. She was kicking the kerbs trying to get loose. Her legs were climbing the wall to get free but she was never going to go anywhere but in

299

a box. Her kicking became less and less till there was no more. I let go and rolled her into the gutter.

"That's where you belong, you scutter."

I lifted the man around so he faced the sky and punched him several times in the neck. I could hear him chocking and blood was coming out of the corner of his mouth.

"You won't be smoking again but it wasn't smoking that killed you."

I dragged him into the gutter next to his accomplice. I looked at them both, laughed and walked into the rear of the hotel. I packed the cases and did a key drop. Then I walked out the front entrance like a normal guest. There was no mercy from Malak as I knew my enemies were not good people and did not deserve any mercy. There would be none given from them. We were at war and in war, people died. I hummed as I walked to the station. It was just another day.

I made my way to the station still humming the same tune as I did when I terminated the photographer. It was not a tune that made you want to sing. It was coming out the mouth of a serial killer. They all thought they were going to kill me. As long as they stayed apart, they were easy pickings. I would terminate the lot of them. I started to put my foot down a bit as it was getting close to meeting Mateo at the station. I wouldn't tell him what happened. I needed him on that train, not in the toilet. I was used to Mateo now. He was not the strongest person. He had a loose stool problem. That's what we used to call it on missions when we killed men and women in front of them.

I came up to the station and I could see Mateo. He was outside with the collar of his coat up looking like a gangster guarding a mafia godfather.

"Have you checked if the train is on time, my love?" I asked.

"It appears to be on time," he said. "There are lots of people inside. I haven't seen any here but there were about three different couples coming up the street, holding back, behind you so as not to get too close."

"Yes," I said, "I was aware they were there. We will stay out here till the train comes and wait for the queue. It will look like we are meeting someone outside the station. Just keep your eye on the arrivals board."

As I finished talking, Mateo spoke in an excited voice, "It's here."

"Be quiet," I said, "Everybody will hear you. It's a covert operation. Talk quietly."

Chapter 49

Mateo

We could see out of the corner of our eyes the queue was going down fast. We could see two rail police with guns at the barriers. We walked at a pace so as not to alarm the police but to get in fast. We showed our tickets and the ticket guard waved us in.

We passed the rail police. Jasmin looked up and they both smiled at her. She was a beautiful woman and had a lot of attention from men and she knew how to extract it. She put her arm in mine and showed them who she belonged to. *Wow*, I thought, *if they only knew what we did they would have shot her at the ticket machine.* Although I was sure she would have gotten them before they could get those guns out. She was like lightning.

We hurried our way onto the train and got a seat, looking out of the window. We could see two men with money out trying to get the guard to let them past the barrier. The guard was pointing to the ticket office, but they were waving their hands and arms around. The police were unclipping their guns and their hands were on the handles of the guns ready to draw.

Jasmin was laughing her head off. She had fooled them and she was one step ahead of them now but we were not sure if they had more people that could board before Dijon. The train pulled out, and we were on our way. Jasmin kissed me.

"My darling, I love you," she said.

"I love you more," I replied and we held each other tightly. We were still so in love. We had come a long way in our battle for freedom but we would have a rest till we got into Dijon. We went to the buffet carriage and got two double expressos; we needed a large fix of caffeine.

We were starting to get into the mountains. The train was climbing on a gradual slope but making way up to a higher altitude. We sat back drinking the coffee. It was nice to be relaxing with my woman. She had sorted out the photographer. He was a bit late with his picture. Jasmin was only protecting us by killing him. To stop more mercenaries coming after us. We should have killed him earlier. We might have been free of them. His actions got us more attention.

Jasmin was cuddling up to me. I was looking at her. She was stunningly beautiful. She was unblemished. She reminded me of the day I met her on the train to Paris. It seemed so long ago but she was as pretty now as then. All the killing had made her more attractive in a savage kind of way. The more I looked at her, the more I fell for her.

This woman, this super woman, was mine. All mine and nobody was going to part us. Bar him up there, our God, if it was his will.

Jasmin was fast off to sleep; I could see a helicopter flying along the side of the train. There were four men including the pilot. They were looking in the windows, flying down from the front to the rear. I woke Jasmin.

"What's wrong?" she said. "Why have you woken me? I was just in a dream."

"You need to wake up, baby. There is a helicopter looking for us outside."

Jasmin looked up fast and said, "Get down. Don't let them see us."

It was too late. One of them was pointing from the helicopter.

"We are in trouble now. They are following us," I said.

The train was speeding along. We could see the peaks of the mountains in front of us and the train was bending towards the large mountain in front. The helicopter was beginning to climb to get over the top of the mountain. I could see a tunnel going through the middle of the mountain.

Jasmin said, "Come on. Let's go into another carriage towards the front. We can at least be out of the firing line if they see us on the other side."

We were getting ready to go through the tunnel, and the helicopter was in the distance going over the top of the mountain.

"We will sit out of sight as they will try and pick us off with a rifle," she said.

We made our way up the carriages. It was a long train with lots of carriages. We had two train engines pulling the carriages. We got near the front. It was a long tunnel. We sat on the opposite side in first class. We came out the tunnel, and the train track in the distance was bending right to another tunnel in the distance.

We could see the helicopter following the track around with the train, coming in close looking for us. They kept on coming in and going out as the train curved following the track. It was difficult as we were really high up on a mountain pass. It had been cut through the mountain. The helicopter was searching and having to go over to come back down to the carriages. We were getting closer to the other tunnel and the helicopter left us again climbing to get on the other side of the tunnel. It was another long tunnel we had to bear. Would they have gone? Probably crashed into the mountain with a bit of luck.

We would be clearing the tunnel soon. We were hoping the helicopter wasn't on the other side; crashed or given up. As we came out, we looked. There was an open stretch to the next tunnel and no obstructions like before. We were on a large bridge stretching between two mountains. As we looked down, it must have been a five thousand foot drop. The helicopter was coming over to the train in the distance. The train was going along fast. The helicopter was trying to meet it before it made it to the next tunnel. We got out of our seats and went to see the helicopter door opening and a man with a rocket launcher pointing out at the train.

"Get down," Jasmin shouted, "They are going to blow the train up."

You could see the missile leave the launcher and shoot like a bullet to the train. There was a massive explosion. The train started to tilt from one side to another. You could hear the brakes coming on the carriages and the noise seemed to go quiet. Then there was a massive noise of metal crashing. We could see the rear carriages going over the side, breaking away from the rest of the train and going into the ravine. The train was not holding the carriages and they had crumpled above the top of the others.

We were okay but we had a massive problem. The weight of the carriages over into the ravine was in danger of pulling the whole train into the ravine with it. There was no real way out. The sheer weight of the carriages would be our Achilles' heel as we would all be doomed to the same fate. The carriages were being pulled off the track one by one. They were going to pull us off in four carriages into the ravine. Once the carriage was over the edge, there would be no coming back. The weight of the carriages was getting heavier by the next carriage. We had to try to get off but the weight of the carriages was taking them off the track.

We never had a chance to get out. We moved to the rear of the carriage hoping we could get out the door before it joined the others over the side. We could feel it slipping off the track. There was no time for anything now but goodbyes. We hung onto the seat. The carriage was going over with us in it and people were being thrown out into the front that was now nearly vertical over the side of the mountain.

All of a sudden, there was a loud creak and the sound of ripping metal. The weight of the carriages connected to ours had pulled our carriage apart and the carriages were on their way down five thousand feet. People were dropping out the bottom of the carriage to their deaths along with all the others. The carriage moved and we lost our grip and sped down the carriage to the open end. Jasmin twisted, blocking the corridor. I crashed into her. She started to slide out the carriage. I just managed to catch her arm.

But I could not hold her. She was in the air five thousand feet above the ground. I could feel the weight of her plus the gravity of her. She was a dead weight. I was not going to be able to hold her, but I had to. Even if she ripped my arm off with her as she fell to her death. She was hanging there. She had managed to hold my hand but it would not be any help as I was struggling to hold her. And she was slipping.

"Don't let go," Jasmin said, crying, "Please hold me, baby. Hold me, hold me. I don't want to die. I need to live. Save us both. I'm pregnant. Don't let us go, Mateo. I love you! Help me!"

Lightning Source UK Ltd.
Milton Keynes UK
UKHW041500220422
401704UK00012B/43